PRAISE FOR "THE UNLIVED LIVES OF RAYMOND QUINN"

Many thanks to the readers who took the time to review *The Unlived Lives of Raymond Quinn*, the first book in the "Unlived Lives" series.

"Perfect for anyone who likes a bit of everything—philosophy, adventure, and a good, page-turning plot. One of my top books for 2024..."

"Very interesting and intriguing delve into alternative lives emanating from one young man's tragic demise during the war in Vietnam."

"This is an excellent story to read about life decisions, second chances and one that will have you thinking about your own life choices."

"The author explores complex themes including life and death, the afterlife, and the rippling consequences of our decisions."

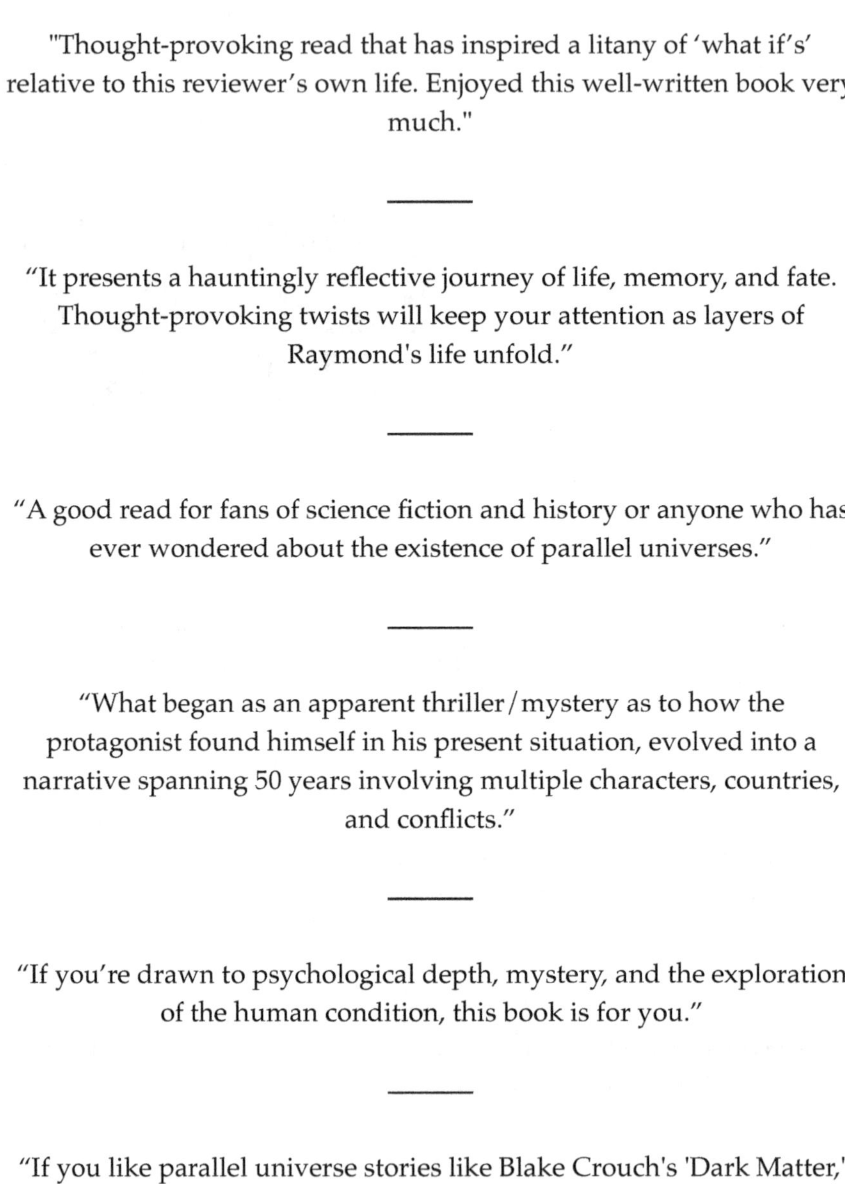

"Thought-provoking read that has inspired a litany of 'what if's' relative to this reviewer's own life. Enjoyed this well-written book very much."

"It presents a hauntingly reflective journey of life, memory, and fate. Thought-provoking twists will keep your attention as layers of Raymond's life unfold."

"A good read for fans of science fiction and history or anyone who has ever wondered about the existence of parallel universes."

"What began as an apparent thriller/mystery as to how the protagonist found himself in his present situation, evolved into a narrative spanning 50 years involving multiple characters, countries, and conflicts."

"If you're drawn to psychological depth, mystery, and the exploration of the human condition, this book is for you."

"If you like parallel universe stories like Blake Crouch's 'Dark Matter,' you need to meet Raymond Quinn."

This is a work of fiction. Names, characters, places, and incidents either are the product of the author's imagination or are used fictitiously. Any resemblance to actual persons, living or dead, events, or locales is entirely coincidental.

Paperback: 979-8-9909986-4-3

Ebook: 979-8-9909986-5-0

Audiobook available on Audible.

CREDITS

Cover design: Paula L. Johnson Creative Services

Cover image: Maximusnd

Page design: Vellum

Proofreading: Flo Selfman

Dog tag art: Kyle Matthies

Author jacket photo: Skye Moorhead

Audiobook narration: JT Farrell

WilliamMatthies.com

Published by William Matthies

THE UNLIVED LIVES: RECKONING

UNLIVED LIVES · BOOK 3

WILLIAM MATTHIES

"There are two things you should remember when dealing with parallel universes. One, they're not really parallel, and two, they're not really universes."

Douglas Adams, British science fiction writer

PROLOGUE

"MY NAME WAS ĐOÀN ĂN GIÁP. I WAS VIETNAMESE. I WAS A SOLDIER during the Chiến tranh kháng chiến chống lại Mỹ, Vietnamese for Resistance War against America, in what Americans called the North Vietnamese Army. The Vietnamese name was Quân Đội Đội ân Dân Việt Nam—in English, the People's Army of Vietnam."

How long ago?

A corridor lined in wood, infused with centuries of incense, recalling a bygone era, leading to a room meant only for one. Nothing on the walls other than a single mirror reflecting an expressionless face. Sometimes a sanctuary, sometimes a prison. Giáp enters, his existence complete except for...

The war no longer matters; it all happened so long ago. You now exist to help others discover where they are meant to be. You know what they don't. They are dead, you are dead, and they must find their eternal, infinite, immortal existence. You will help guide them to that.

Sitting on his plank bed, the rank odor of musk rising from his clothes, hinting at death long passed, he wondered.

Why not me as well?

Look behind you, Giáp, at the wall. What is its purpose? Is it meant to keep you in or others out? Which is it, Giáp? Why have you not questioned the wall?

Giáp turned slowly. The wall, now almost translucent, beckoned him to enter through an opening seemingly too small for him to pass through. He questioned, *Where to do what?*

Faintly at first, getting louder, a voice whispered his name.

"Come, Giáp, your time is now. Come with me, I will take you."

The voice sounded like his own, like that of Raymond Quinn, like Shelly Bennett.

He stood, taller than the opening, moving slowly toward the wall, entering another time and place.

CHAPTER ONE

You insisted that Raymond be at Other Worlds with you and Don. Why weren't you there?

Must there be a reason for everything?

Yes, but in many cases, including this one, we often don't want to admit what is so obvious to others. You have glimpsed only a small fraction of the countless lives you could have lived. You acknowledged they weren't what you wanted your eternal life to be. You had valid reasons for not choosing them. Do you feel the same about this last one?

Good reasons? We're talking about how my soul will exist forever. Do you want me to pick one of the few lives I might have lived had I made different choices? You tell me to choose carefully. And now, for the first time, you ask if I have good reasons for not *choosing one unlived life. What makes whichever life I choose so special?*

I am you, Shelly; you know everything you need to know. The only difference is that I acknowledge what you prefer to hide from yourself. You are choosing an eternal future for your immortal soul. I have told you to do so carefully. You know what you must do, but you haven't admitted to yourself what that is. Until you do, your soul will not find rest.

Shelly's second trip to Antigua, this time without Raymond, wasn't quite what she had expected. Her age, along with memories of both of them being much younger, led her to question why she had returned to Antigua.

What did I expect? I'm older now, and Raymond is too, assuming he's even alive.

She went through the motions of a tropical beach holiday, swimming, sunning, and snorkeling. But everything reminded her of her first trip, almost twenty years earlier.

I didn't appreciate everything we shared back then, but I do now. It's not the same without him. And now, whether I want to or not, I have the strangest dreams about him almost every night. He talks to me. He wakes me up, and I know I am not asleep. He asks me questions. I answer him. If that's not true, I must be losing my mind.

Shelly convinced herself this was real; she and Raymond were connecting through their dreams. But she wouldn't tell anyone for fear of seeming crazy.

Shelly's last day at the beach ended, and she headed back to the hostel to prepare for her final night in Antigua. Susan and Anne had left the day before, and while she enjoyed their company, she also valued the peace of her alone time in the room they shared. One last night—dinner alone at Caribbean Pisano—and then it was time to leave... She couldn't say to what or where.

I could have stayed here a few more days, but why? It wasn't the same with Susan and Anne. Better than being alone, but I am ready to leave. Too many ghosts of my first trip with Raymond.

"Will your friends be with you again tonight, Shelly?" Enrique, the waiter who served the three of them during their two visits to Pisano, asked as he walked to the same table they had sat at before.

"No, just me tonight. They left for home yesterday. I'm leaving tomorrow."

"Sad to see you all go; you had so much fun together. I enjoyed serving you."

"Thank you, Enrique. We enjoyed your company too. We referred to you as our first and only 'boyfriend' on this trip." Seeing him blush, Shelly added, "Oh, come on, Enrique, you knew we were flirting with you, and not just because you were the only guy around who paid any attention to us. Three older women, we made the best of it, and you loved the attention."

Thoroughly embarrassed, Enrique fumbled to open the menu and handed it to Shelly.

"Can I get you a Wadadli?"

"I thought you'd never ask, and keep an eye on my glass. When it's close to empty, bring me another."

Shelly drank beer with Susan and Anne, but tonight she did so because she was afraid of being alone. She didn't intend to get drunk, but she wouldn't go to bed completely sober.

Raymond, if I dream of you again tonight, I don't want to feel sad. Being alone is one thing; feeling sad and alone is another. It's better to be slightly drunk and asleep.

But Shelly wasn't getting the pleasure she expected from drinking, nor did she enjoy dinner. She finished, stood up to leave, and thanked Enrique, hugging him. The two of them said they looked forward to seeing each other again on her next trip to Five Islands Village. Shelly wasn't sure if Enrique honestly thought she would come again. She knew she wouldn't.

CHAPTER TWO

Back in her hostel room, alone, Shelly looked around, making sure to gather all her belongings as she packed for her departure the next morning.

Why is packing to go home always more difficult than packing to leave home? Sad, too, knowing I will likely never be back here again.

Her things in order, she set an alarm for 7:00 AM, leaving time for a quick breakfast before the short walk to the shuttle that would take her back to V.C. Bird Airport. Everything ready, now in bed, she soon fell asleep.

Was it worth the trip? Would you do it again?

I'm not sure. I'm disappointed you weren't with me. However, I might have been more disappointed had you been here.

Really? How so?

You have to know, Raymond. We are dead! We 'encounter' each other, but we are not together. What kind of relationship is that? And now in these crazy dreams I'm having. If this is to be our immortal 'unlived lives', what is the point?

These dreams might lead us to something else, Shelly. Something more real than our lives were before we died.

Do you honestly think so? I don't. We spent time together as kids in Antigua and later, after the war, as young adults in Vietnam. We travelled together through Europe, ultimately to Zimbabwe, and you know how that ended. You also know, none of that happened. Asian made it clear that we were experiencing bits and pieces of lives we could have lived had we made different choices. That's not life.

I don't know what I know, but what if our eternity is just what you said? What do we do then? You are not happy, but you should consider how much worse things could have been. Shelly, wake up!

As if shaken by an unseen force, Shelly sat up in bed, seeing nothing in the dark room. She turned on the bedside lamp, looking around as if she expected someone to be there.

That was Raymond. I remember everything we said. He's reaching out to me. Does he know I am awake?

"Raymond, talk to me. I dreamed we were talking, it was too real for us not to be."

What would I do if he talked to me? Ghosts don't speak; they keep people awake at night. But I wasn't awake, I was sleeping, dreaming. Every night, I dream he is talking to me, and not about what has happened to each of us separately. We discuss us as a couple. Maybe he is right. We could be living our eternal lives. If so, at least we are together in some way.

And what if that is your eternal unlived life? Would that satisfy you?

It would have to if that's all there is.

Pay close attention. What we say to each other in those dreams is important. They form the foundation of our eternal lives.

CHAPTER THREE

"COME IN, RAY, SIT DOWN."

Unsure where he was, Raymond did as the voice instructed.

"What is this place?" Looking for something he recognized, he finally saw Asian.

"It doesn't matter, Ray. What matters is that we are together again to finish what we started. You ask questions, searching for answers, and now you are questioning this place. What do you see?"

Raymond looked around, hoping to see something familiar.

"I will tell you, Ray. We are an anomaly—a product of our two minds working separately and together. There are no walls, no floor, and no ceiling—just you, the American soldier, and me, the NVA soldier, no longer enemies. Notice the smell, Ray? Burning human waste. Are you surprised that your enemy's body waste, once burned, smells just like yours? Two opposing soldiers, so different, yet not different at all, on this basic human trait. Isn't it time to reflect, not on our differences but instead, on what makes us the same?"

Looking around, Ray saw shapes form and change, colors separate and converge to create new shades he had never seen before; all this, along with a somewhat comforting low-frequency hum, made him feel at ease. He hadn't felt this way when he first met Asian. But so much had happened since then, and was happening now; he accepted it.

"I'm here for a reason, aren't I, Asian?

"Yes, you are. Do you know what that reason is?"

"Shelly's dreams?"

"Do you know what that means?"

"Shelly and I have contacted each other. We are communicating with each other."

"You are not certain of that, but yes, you are. And while Shelly thinks so too, she also has doubts. She wakes up hearing you reply, believing that proves you are communicating. However, as you will soon learn, your dreams aren't the only way you can speak to each other."

"She wants to know if this is the alternative life we are both destined to live? Is speaking to each other in our dreams as together as we will ever be? If I am talking to Shelly while dreaming, I need to know."

"All you've learned about your immortal existence, you've discovered on your own. I've told you nothing, taught you nothing. There is no end to the process of discovery. You gain knowledge without ever knowing certainty, but you can learn from your dreams. Live them, Ray. Tell Shelly she must do the same. You could have returned to your unhappy existence, but no longer. Accept that, and you will continue to learn more."

CHAPTER FOUR

SHELLY, I'VE BEEN WITH ASIAN AGAIN. HE SAID WE ARE EVOLVING. Our immortal lives are not settled, our relationship is not yet determined. We must pay attention to our dreams.

Someone else said something very similar. 'These are not simply dreams, Shelly; they are the basis for the rest of our eternal lives.' That was you, Raymond. We are talking to each other in our dreams!

Yes, but what does that accomplish?

You also said, 'What we say to each other in those dreams is important.' We communicate with one another. This will lead us to the immortal, unlived lives we both want to experience. Isn't that what Asian is telling you?

What do we want, Shelly? We know what we don't have, but what do we truly want? That is what we should dream about. Our future, not our past. I want contentment and peace of mind, taking responsibility for what I can, accepting what I cannot. But how do we know what that is?

I don't know, Raymond, but at least we have a starting point. We are experiencing something extraordinary. Previously, I thought our immortal existences would be similar to our mortal lives. Possibly less threatening, less complicated, but more similar than not. Now I see it is much more than that.

Ok, but what do we dream about? It can't be material things; as you said, we are dead.

Shelly smiled to herself. "It hadn't occurred to me until now that what was important to me when I was alive might not be the same when I was dead. But I know that now. That is progress, and speaking of which, I'm telling you this now, not dreaming it. Do you hear me, Ray? I am not dreaming."

In separate parts of the multiverse, light-years of time apart, possibly for eternity, they suddenly found themselves able to communicate as though both were in the same room.

"I hear you, Shelly. Other than a few short letters, there's never been an 'us' in mortal life, only our strange 'encounters'. The first after my death, five years later after yours, all in our unlived lives. But as Asian often says to me, we are blessed to have this renewed chance at immortal life. I never fully understood what he meant by that. I do now. We must not waste this, Shelly. We have to define 'contentment' and 'peace of mind' to have a chance of achieving it."

Shelly heard every word Ray said, realizing she also knew what he would say before he spoke.

"Our communication is complex, no longer constrained by time or space. And if that's true for you, tell me what I'm thinking right now, Ray."

Choosing not to speak, Ray answered in thought.

It means there are no limits to what we can accomplish. It means we are together across the entire multiverse. Asian never said this would happen, but he knew it would. He read my thoughts. He had reached a level of being unavailable to mortals, and only a few, including us, have achieved it.

For the first time, both understood their immortal unlived lives began the moment each of their mortal lives ended. The task before them now was to define what they would do, separately and together.

CHAPTER FIVE

Asian?

Yes.

Raymond looked around, expecting to find himself in Other Worlds with Asian, possibly including the barista. Instead, he was in a completely different place. A room of sorts, but like no other he had experienced. The walls shifted colors, moving so slowly that he hadn't initially noticed. The air was pleasantly fresh, as though outdoors, with a comforting scent that reminded him of light incense without smoke. No tables, chairs, no barista or customers, and no Asian. A low musical hum throughout the room. Without knowing where he was or why, Raymond sensed he was where he should be.

"You asked to meet and talk."

Raymond recognized the voice as Asian. He saw a blurry image of him emerging through the walls around him, growing closer. Finally, they were sitting comfortably in chairs that hadn't been there before.

"Yes, I did, Asian."

"Will this discussion begin where our last left off?"

"No, it will not; too much has changed for that to happen. I understand what I did not before. I've accepted being dead. I know I have visited lives I might have lived had I made different choices, including two with Shelly. You made it clear that I had to select the one person I wanted my eternal, unlived life to be with. I chose Shelley. I assumed I would find something that appeared to be very similar to the mortal life I thought I had been living. Maybe that will still be the case, but as of this moment, I doubt that it will."

"Do you have some idea what it will be, possibly what you would like it to be?"

"What it will be, yes. What it will be like, I'm not sure. Shelly and I are communicating through thought and voice. Clearly communicating. She may be able to hear or sense what I am saying to you now. She has recently."

"Recently? A way you marked time in your mortal life. Time as you once knew it no longer applies to you, Ray. All measurements of time are now meaningless to you, Shelly, and me. We have all the time in the world and no time at all for eternity."

Raymond considered what Asian said before responding.

"As much as I have learned, there is so much I don't know. Isn't that so, Asian?"

"Not so much what you don't know as it is the need to acknowledge your new reality. Please excuse the expression; that will take time, Ray."

"Shelly and I have entered a new dimension of existence. We are not what we were, and we are not yet what we will eventually become."

Looking around at the translucent color-shifting walls, Raymond continued.

"Wherever I am now is a fitting representation of our questions. What is this place? What am I? What is Shelly? Will we find answers to these questions and more, and if so, when? What can we do to accelerate our learning?"

"Start by not concerning yourself with time-related change. 'When', 'how long', 'accelerate' have no meaning for you. However, I will provide a partial answer to your questions. When we first met, do you recall struggling to accept me saying you were dead and had been for over forty-six years? Do you recall being unable to process lost time at Other Worlds, including how and when you went home at night, when you came back the next day, always finding yourself sitting in one of the chairs, not knowing when or even if you had left?"

Raymond knew that everything Asian said to him carried meaning. But being reminded of their first meeting, forced to accept his mortal death once more, took Ray back to a time and place he hoped he would never revisit.

"I do, although I wish I didn't. It still bothers me."

"And it will until you find it no longer does. You are glad you and Shelly are emerging from a very dark place to one more promising. That is real, but you have much to learn to complete the process. If you wish, as you call it, to 'accelerate' what you still must learn, remind yourself that time is no longer a dimension for you. It may seem a small matter, but doing so will help you. Eventually, the beginning of this transformation will fade from your memory."

"I understand, but is there anything more you can tell me? Something I can share with Shelly, that we should or should not do during this transitional process?"

"Nothing you do not already know."

You will know when it is time to leave a place, person, or situation. Do not minimize the importance of what you choose. Do not put off deciding to change something you know is wrong. Doing so is a decision the consequences of which will end your ability to choose your immortal life.

CHAPTER SIX

"ASIAN AND I TALKED. HE CONFIRMED WHAT WE SUSPECTED. WE ARE transitioning from our mortal lives to our immortal existences. He said we should not think in terms of time, a dimension that no longer applies to us. We have as much time, or no time, to become whatever it is we want to be, together or apart. We will slowly become more comfortable with our new reality."

Shelly listened carefully, hearing but not fully understanding what this meant. However, she had an immediate question for Raymond.

"You said, '... to become whatever it is we want to be together or apart'. What do you mean by that, Raymond? I thought we were together as we briefly were in our mortal lives, and in our search for each other after death. We were for me, not for you? Shouldn't you at least be certain about that much as you attempt to transition to your immortal life?"

Raymond heard what Shelly said, her words devoid of any emotion.

True in Antigua when we were young, later in Vietnam, Europe, and Zimbabwe, which did not end well. You said you would go with me to Germany. You didn't, nor did you tell me that you wouldn't. We did better in Vietnam and Europe, both mostly on your terms. And finally, in Zimbabwe, until you ordered me to leave your apartment. We are in transition, is our relationship as well?

Having heard Raymond's thoughts, Shelly responded.

"I understand our history might make you question our future together. All you think now happened in the past. What did Asian tell you about that? Isn't that part of the time dimension that shouldn't concern us? Remember, Raymond, neither of us knew then what we know now. If you had known you were the other Raymond, killed in the war, what would that have meant for us? I'll answer for you; we wouldn't be having this conversation now. It would have meant you lied to me. I now know you didn't. You said and acted based on what you believed to be true. Now we both understand everything about each other's actions. There are no lies in the multiverse; we each hear what the other says and thinks. I hear you now, but I want you to tell me—will we be together? Do you want to spend eternity with me?"

"Shelly, everything you've said is true. It's also true that I haven't said or thought whether we would be together in the multiverse. All of this is very new to both of us, so we can't know that yet. You remember your time in London with Lionel and the impulsive decision you made to move to Israel. At some point, everyone acts too quickly based on limited knowledge. Aside from that, did you ever consider our brief communication before I was killed, and how you committed suicide five years later? If you didn't, was it because our relationship no longer mattered to you? That happened because our unlived lives overlapped. We are only now beginning what will be our eternal futures, with perfect memory of our imperfect mortal pasts. You want me to tell you whether I want us to be together in the multiverse. I already have."

And you both hear my thoughts as well. I am your conscience. I now compel both of you to be honest about what you think, say, and do. You have reached a different stage, evolving from mortal to immortal lives. You have an excellent opportunity to contemplate your immortal futures, trying to shape them into nearly anything you want, alone or together. You started this transformation and discovery process positively, able to communicate with each other—something you could not do before your mortal deaths. Shelly, you now demand assurances from Raymond that he cannot give you. She is to be forgiven for that, Raymond, because you refuse even to try to focus on what Shelly asks of you. Your indecisiveness is at the core of Shelly's concern about a future with you. And yes, Shelly, you are not confident enough to conclude that your immortal future is with Raymond. You choose not to focus on that, instead ignoring the question, so Raymond will not see how uncertain you are. What will you both do now? Start again, each of you focusing on what you want, not on what the other can or cannot provide. Decide what that is, and then look to each other to see if your needs and desires align.

One more thing.

Raymond, I come to you as Đoàn ăn Giáp, the NVA soldier you killed—the same one who killed you. Shelly, you know me as your conscience, urging you to face what you hope to hide from yourself and others. I am neither solely that nor solely this; I am both. Like you, I am a soul in the multiverse seeking my forever. Unlike you, I do not hide anything from myself or others. I am telling you this now because, in the past, you would not have accepted this truth. If you continue to ignore or refuse my guidance, either knowingly or unknowingly, you will learn nothing more about your immortal futures. You have made solid progress understanding what you seek, but not enough—definitely not all you need to know.

Think carefully about what this means; it has everything to do with both your futures. Begin by reflecting on the impact that Singapore has had on both of you and your relationship. You cannot do this together; you must do it separately. You, Shelly, by revisiting Singapore as you did before you committed suicide. You, Raymond, searching for what you would have found had you not been killed. After you have done that, search for meaning for both of you based on what you have learned.

You will know when it is time to leave a place, person, or situation. Do not minimize the importance of what you choose. Do not put off deciding to change something you know is wrong. Doing so is a decision the consequences of which will end your ability to choose your immortal life.

CHAPTER SEVEN

Over thirty hours of travel time, but I'll be there soon. Raymond will be waiting for me. I can't wait to meet him.

Raymond and Shelly knew each other based on nothing more than a few letters. Shelly understood this and was enthusiastic about meeting Raymond in person, happy to accept whatever came of their time together.

I hope he isn't disappointed in me. I've only sent him one picture. More than just appearances will determine what happens. Who knows? This trip might be much shorter than either of us expected, at least for me. Whether he likes me or not, he'll have to stay for a week regardless.

The plane landed at Paya Lebar Airport, and shortly after, Shelly waited anxiously for her luggage before heading through immigration and customs. Sleeping more than she expected after the second and final refueling stopover, she was ready to meet Raymond.

The flight wasn't full, and since only two other flights were landing within half an hour, she quickly went through immigration and customs, and was released to the greeting area for arriving passengers. One last door to go through; she took a deep breath.

This is it. Get ready, Raymond!

She looked for a US soldier uniform, assuming that was what he would be wearing. Seeing none among the hundreds meeting arriving planes, Shelly walked toward the exit gate. When he didn't appear, she waited, thinking he might be on his way, a little late due to traffic. Half an hour passed, still waiting, unsure of what to do. She tried to recall whether he had said he would meet her at the airport or at the Raffles Hotel, where they had booked rooms. Seeing no alternative, she decided to take a taxi to the hotel.

Traffic was relatively light mid-morning, and Shelly reached the hotel in less than forty minutes. The bellman took her luggage and told her he would bring it to the front desk. She entered the lobby, looking left and right for anyone she thought might be Raymond, but saw no one.

"Yes, miss, may I help you?"

"I have a reservation under Shelly Bennett. Can you check if I have any messages?"

"Certainly, king size, one guest, checking out next Thursday, the fourteenth. I'll check for messages," the clerk said, turning toward the area behind him. "No messages," he added, waving to the bellman with her suitcase and shoulder bag. "Room 306; enjoy your stay."

Disappointed and tired, Shelly's only option was to follow the bellman to her room and wait for word from Raymond.

Did I misunderstand something? I'm sure he said he would meet me at the airport. Maybe the front desk can tell me something about his reservation.

After the bellman left, she picked up the receiver and dialed the front desk. Two rings later, she recognized the desk clerk's voice. "Front desk. May I help you, Miss Bennett?"

"Hopefully, you can. I am supposed to meet another guest here, Mr. Raymond Quinn. You might have him registered by his US Army rank. Can you tell me if he has checked in?"

"Please hold, I will check."

A few moments later, the desk clerk came back on the line."

"We have a reservation for Corporal Raymond Quinn, guaranteed for late arrival yesterday. He hasn't checked in yet. Would you like to leave a message for when he does?"

"Yes, tell him I am here, please call my room."

"I will. Is there anything more I can do for you, Miss Bennett?"

"No, thank you, that's all for now. Just make sure he gets my message."

"I will certainly do that. Goodbye."

Shelly hung up the receiver, feeling sad and a little worried as she wondered what else she could do to learn more.

He's not at the airport to meet me; no message. The hotel still has a reservation for him. At least I know he planned to be here. If not, why keep a hotel reservation? If he decided not to come, he would have canceled it. Maybe he's staying at another hotel? If so, to avoid being close to me? No, something must have happened before he left the war.

Not knowing what else she could do, with no one to call, Shelly took a shower, dressed, and spent the afternoon waiting to see if Raymond arrived or left a message for her. She was tired but too worried and anxious to sleep. She stayed in her room for a couple of hours before deciding to wait in the lobby, hoping to see him walk through the front door. Once downstairs, she checked the front desk again to see if she might have missed his arrival while coming down from her room. No message, and he had not checked in. The clerk said they would have to release his reservation if there were guests requesting a room.

Shelly waited, reading *The Straits Times,* the country's leading English-language newspaper. She remembered being in school, forced to read something she found dull. Her eyes would move over the words, but her brain barely retained any of it. That was happening now, but not out of boredom. Shelly was growing more worried about Raymond, unsure of what to do if she didn't hear anything about him.

The afternoon ended, and she had dinner at the hotel, or at least ordered it. She had little appetite, despite having last eaten on the plane. Once the waiter cleared her dishes, she went back to the front desk to check if there were any messages. Nothing.

What should I do now? I have no reason to believe he will come. If he doesn't show up tonight and I don't hear from him tomorrow, what then?

Back in her room, fatigue finally overtook her concern for Raymond and herself, and she fell asleep in her clothes, not waking until six-thirty the next morning.

"Good morning, Miss Bennett, how can I help you?" the morning desk clerk, a different one from the day before, asked after answering her call.

"Are there any messages for me or news about Corporal Raymond Quinn? He was scheduled to arrive two days ago. He has a reservation here at the hotel. We were to meet here, and I haven't heard anything from or about him since I arrived yesterday."

"Just a moment, I'll check."

A few moments later, he came back on the line.

"No messages from or regarding Corporal Quinn, and we had to release his reservation to another guest."

"Thank you," Shelly said, hanging up the receiver.

She looked around the room as if expecting to find something that would help her decide what to do. She had booked the room for five nights and could stay, enjoying her time as a tourist. She quickly dismissed the thought. Even the idea of enjoying herself alone repelled her.

I have no idea why he's not here, whether he's coming, or what I should do. Do what, be a tourist? Absolutely not! I will stay one more night, and if I haven't heard from him by late this afternoon, I will book a return flight home.

Shelly was angry at Raymond and herself for being so, knowing he was in a war and could be injured or dead.

But there's nothing I can do about it. Once I'm back home, he might write to explain... assuming he's able to write.

With no word from or about Raymond the next morning and early afternoon, Shelly rebooked herself on a 1:00 AM departure the next day, retracing her thirty-plus-hour journey back to Harare.

CHAPTER EIGHT

You knew, didn't you, Shelly?

That he was dead? No, I didn't. I couldn't allow myself to think that. If I had, I wouldn't have gone looking for him in Seattle.

You knew, Shelly, during those nights alone in Singapore.

I di… Oh God, yes, I did, but I could not allow myself to accept that he was. I needed to hang onto hope that he was alive and well somewhere.

And during your second trip to Antigua, this one alone, did you think he might be alive somewhere then?

Possibly, I don't know. I preferred not to think about any of that while I was with Anne and Susan.

But thinking about it has always been what you should be doing. Raymond certainly is, even more so now, having learned the details of your time in Singapore. It's the result of both of you now being able to communicate with each other in thought and speech. And you will soon learn what he thinks of that place, you—the person—and the situation as you experienced it. When he does, once you know, you both will have much to discuss.

CHAPTER NINE

WHAT DO YOU THINK OF SHELLY'S TIME ALONE IN SINGAPORE, WAITING TO hear from or about you?

It felt like I was hearing about someone else. I had to keep reminding myself she was waiting for me. I couldn't control the situation. There was nothing I could do for her. She waited in the lobby, looking up whenever someone entered to see if it was me. All those times she asked the desk clerk if there were any messages for her. Messages from me. I actually thought there might be. But then I reminded myself that wasn't possible. All of this happened more than forty-six years ago.

Would you have been there with her if you hadn't been killed?

Yes, absolutely. I was scheduled to leave on R&R two days after I was killed. Of course I would have gone.

Would you like to experience what that time in Singapore would have been like had you not been killed?

Is that possible?

You can, if you choose to. It is a portion of one of your unlived lives. But understand, not only will you experience it, Shelly will too, just as you experienced her time alone in Singapore. Neither of you can hide or alter anything that happened during your time alone. Everything you say and think will be the truth. You cannot lie, change, or hide any of it. I don't need to ask if you understand and accept these conditions. I don't need to ask if you wish to experience what would have been your time in Singapore with Shelly had you not been killed in the war. I know you do; Shelly does too.

CHAPTER TEN

Exactly as I pictured her. Beautiful!

"Shelly, over here!" Raymond yelled, waving his hands above his head to stand out from the hundred or so others around him, all trying to get the attention of those they had been waiting for at Paya Lebar Airport, Singapore.

Shelly looked around, overwhelmed by the chaos, as she tried to spot someone she thought was Raymond.

If only I had a photograph of him. He said he would send one, but so far, nothing. I hope he can find me.

Hearing her name called, Shelly looked to the far left and saw a young man in civilian clothes waving his arms, pointing at her and himself.

"Raymond?" she whispered to herself.

She quickly walked his direction, suddenly realizing she didn't know what to do in a situation such as this.

We've never met. He has a photo of me, but I had no idea what he looked like until now. What should I say?

Now, through the exit into the crowd waiting for their friends and family, Raymond approached her.

"I assume you are Shelly?"

"I am, and you are Raymond."

“Yes, I am, Shelly. Let me take your bags and step over here to the side for a few moments, away from the crowd.”

Shelly followed Raymond, thinking to herself, *What do we do? Do we hug, shake hands? This is so awkward.*

Raymond set her bags down.

"I'm so happy to see you. You are even prettier than your picture!”

Shelly blushed.

“I always pictured you in some kind of uniform, as you mentioned a few times in your letters—dirty, with a rifle or some kind of weapon," looking him up and down, “not dressed in a shirt and slacks.”

Raymond laughed. "That never occurred to me, but it does make sense. We have so little to go on, just what we've said in a few letters. And now here we are, each of us halfway around the world from our homes. Well, you anyway; I'm close to the war I have to go back to in a week. I hope you're not disappointed. I'm certainly not."

"Oh, no, Raymond, not at all, quite the opposite. You have to forgive me. I am so tired after more than thirty hours of traveling to get here. But all that's behind me now," she said, motioning to the immigration and customs area she had just come from, hoping Raymond found this humorous. "You are definitely *not* a disappointment!"

Laughing again, Raymond replied, "Of course, you would be tired. Let's go to the hotel. I'm checked in, and your room is waiting. After you have time to unpack and do whatever else you'd like, we can meet to plan our time together."

"Sounds good to me. You lead, I'll follow."

Shelly and Raymond exited the airport arrival area and quickly got into a taxi heading to Raffles. As the taxi navigated through busy streets filled with all kinds of vehicles, from cars to human-powered rickshaws, Raymond began to speak.

“I'd like to explain what you're seeing, but I only caught a glimpse of it myself when I arrived and again this morning on my way to meet you at the airport.”

If he only knew I don't care what we see or do. I'm just so happy we're both here, about to spend a wonderful week together.

"Not a problem. You never led me to believe you were a travel guide," she said, looking at him. "Raymond, thank you for meeting me at the airport, and for suggesting we be together this week on your... What do they call it, your war holiday?"

Raymond laughed out loud. "War holiday I'll have to remember that—the guys in my unit will find that very funny. It's called R&R, which stands for rest and relaxation. A holiday, or vacation, as we would call it in the States. Whatever you call it, away from the war is exactly what it is." Looking directly at Shelly, he continued, "I'm thrilled that you agreed to meet me here. I know it must be a great expense and risk, given how little we know of each other. Not so much for me. I had to go somewhere for R&R, and Singapore appealed to me. No transportation expense; the army pays for that. This would be a great break from the war, regardless, but it means so much to me that you will share it with me. Thank you, Shelly."

They arrived at Raffles, and Raymond carried Shelly's luggage inside for her as she completed the check-in process. Shelly in room 306, just down the hall from Raymond in 314.

"I don't know much about the city, but I do know the elevator is off to our left," he said, smiling, as he picked up Shelly's suitcase.

Once in Shelly's room, Raymond said, "I'll give you time to get settled. Call me when you have. I'm in 314. I'll come up with a dinner option. If that doesn't sound good to you, we'll find something else."

"Sounds great. First, I need a hot shower and clean clothes. I can be ready in an hour."

"Not a problem if you need more time or just want to rest before going out."

"Rest would be nice, but I don't want to waste a minute. I'll sleep later."

Raymond left Shelly's room, returning to his own to look for places nearby to eat.

I can't believe we're actually here together. She is beautiful, and I like what little I know of her. I hope she feels the same about me. We should have dinner early; she must be very tired.

Shelly unpacked, took a shower, and got dressed for what she assumed would be a casual dinner.

I never thought to ask how dressed I should be. I'll wear something similar to how he's dressed, hoping he doesn't change.

A little more than an hour later, Raymond dialed Shelly's room.

"Hi, Raymond."

"What if it wasn't me calling?"

"A little embarrassing, but not knowing a single other person in this town, I thought it was a reasonable assumption."

"Are you hungry?"

"I am. I had a good breakfast, but no lunch."

Do you like Chinese food?"

"I love it!"

"Great, I have a reservation in an hour at Spring Court, one of Singapore's oldest restaurants. Not far from here, walkable, but I do enough of that in Vietnam, and it's too muggy here. We'll take a taxi there and back. How about a drink in the hotel's Long Bar? A Singapore Sling, invented here almost one hundred years ago."

"Singapore Sling, huh? What's in it?"

"Lemon juice, dry gin, cherry brandy. I can tell you from my extensive personal knowledge, having been here less than one day more than you, it's quite good."

"What is that saying, 'When in Rome, do as the Romans do'? Something like that. One more question: what does muggy mean?"

Raymond laughed.

"I assumed everyone would know all the words I know. Muggy means too humid, which we would realize if we walked to the restaurant."

"Interesting. Muggy or mugged is British slang for taking advantage of someone, which you would never do to me, would you, Raymond?"

"No, of course not, you can trust me. Now, how about that drink in the Long Bar in, say, ten minutes?"

"Sounds great, I'll be there."

CHAPTER ELEVEN

Raymond was sitting at the bar when Shelly walked in, her Singapore Sling waiting for her.

“I hope you don't mind; I ordered it for you. You don't have to finish it if you don't like it."

“I'm not much of a drinker. But given my British upbringing, and the fact that gin is a close second to tea as England’s national drink, how could I not try it? Cheers!" she said, raising her glass in a toast.

Raymond touched his glass to Shelly's.

“Cheers to you, Shelly, and our time together in Singapore. I hope it's the start of something very special for both of us.”

After taking a sip, Shelly responded.

"Oh, that is good. Maybe I need to become more of a drinker."

“I've reached similar conclusions about different drinks before, only to regret it the next morning. But not this one, this night, with you.”

After finishing their cocktails, they flagged a taxi and arrived at Spring Court restaurant in time for their five o’clock reservation.

Their conversation during dinner mainly involved sharing stories about themselves, their lives, and their hopes for the future. For Shelly, this related to finding a place to live outside Zimbabwe. Raymond was glad to hear this.

She might be happy living in the US with me if our relationship progresses.

"What about you, Raymond? Will you stay in the army?"

"No. I wouldn't even be in it now if it weren't for being drafted. A two-year obligation— by the time I finish my one-year tour in Vietnam, I will only have about six more months before being discharged. After that, I plan to finish college, find a good job, and settle down."

"Seattle, in Washington state? Is that where you want to live after the army?

"It could be. Beautiful country, very green, with generally nice weather if you don't mind a little rain. But I'm open to other areas, especially Southern California. Good weather, beaches nearby. Time will tell. It all depends on the job market at the time."

"California! Everyone knows about California. Movie stars, palm trees. I'd love to go there someday."

Raymond paused before responding, smiling at Shelly.

"Maybe you will. You never know until it happens."

Shelly raised her glass, smiling at Raymond.

"No, Raymond, you never know what might happen. Look at us, in Singapore together. Perfect strangers just a few months ago, and now..." She left the thought unfinished.

Raymond looked at his watch: Seven-thirty.

"What a wonderful evening, made even better being with you, Shelly. You must be tired. Let's head back to the hotel."

"I am tired, but once back, I'd like to talk a little longer if that's all right with you. If I go to bed too early, I might not sleep through the night."

"Certainly, as long as you can stay awake."

Walking into the hotel, Raymond took Shelly's hand. Once inside, he turned to her and said, "Would you like a nightcap?"

"I don't know, what is that?

"Another phrase I supposed everyone knew. Just a way to say, one last drink before going to bed."

"Well, on the one hand, I would, particularly a Singapore Sling. That was so good! But given the first one and wine with dinner, another would certainly put me to sleep. If you're not too tired, how about some more conversation in my room before saying goodnight?"

"I'd love that. Now, *you* lead the way," he said, smiling.

Their conversation continued in Shelly's room, with both describing their hopes for the future. They shared many things in common, like marriage and having a couple of kids, regardless of their gender, as long as they were healthy. The question of where they wanted to live came up again, just as it did at dinner.

"I'm open to many places, as long as I can find a good job in a climate I enjoy, somewhere my wife and family want to be."

"Similar for me, but not in Zimbabwe. There's little opportunity there for women who want to work. Possibly somewhere in the US or the UK if I can be accepted for immigration."

At one point, without the other knowing it, each wanted to say essentially the same thing while questioning whether they should. Shelly was nervous but decided to speak, hoping Raymond would not prefer she hadn't.

"I suppose we should consider going to bed. Are you tired?"

"A little, but not overly so. I don't get enough sleep in Vietnam, given the war, and where we are at times. But you must be exhausted."

"I am, but..." Shelly hesitated, wondering if she would regret speaking openly. She decided she would regret it more the moment he left her room if she didn't.

"...if you don't mind, I'd like you to stay with me tonight, Ray."

CHAPTER TWELVE

Shelly awoke a little after four AM, her jet-lagged mind unadjusted to the time difference between Harare and Singapore. Lying on her side, she momentarily imagined herself back in her apartment, until she opened her eyes and saw her hotel room, her suitcase off to the side of the bed.

Raymond?

As quietly as possible, she rolled onto her back, unsure whether she had dreamed asking him to stay with her. Looking to her left, she saw Raymond still sleeping.

An instant wave of joy and contentment swept over her as she remembered their first night together in Singapore, quickly realizing she couldn't recall how it ended.

He's here, but what did we do? When did I fall asleep? We were talking; I remember that, but for how long?

Needing to use the bathroom but not wanting to wake Raymond, she quietly slipped out of bed, closing the bathroom door behind her. After she finished, she decided to sit in a chair instead of risking waking him while getting back into bed.

He looks so peaceful sleeping. I know he's tired; he needs to rest before heading back to the war.

Less than an hour had passed as Shelly watched Raymond sleep.

Then, as if he had heard a loud noise, he quickly looked around, not noticing her sitting in the chair.

"Good morning, I hope I didn't wake you. I know you're tired—try to go back to sleep; it's still pretty early."

Raymond sat up in bed, smiling.

"Good morning. How did you sleep?"

"Very well, until about an hour ago, when my mind told my body it was time to wake up. Please try to sleep a little longer, Ray; you need the rest."

"Couldn't if I wanted to. There's only a one-hour time difference between Vietnam and Singapore. I'm usually up at this time, having had less sleep than last night. Besides, we only have five days left before we both go back to our normal lives. I loved sleeping with you, but I don't want to miss what we'll do while awake."

Raymond got out of bed somewhat self-conscious, wearing only his army-issued green boxer shorts.

"I'll just be a few minutes," he said, as he went into the bathroom and closed the door behind him."

I'm so happy he agreed to stay last night, but it's clear neither of us considered how awkward the morning after would be. I hope he doesn't regret staying with me.

The bathroom door opened, and Raymond stepped out, smiling at Shelly.

"Ok, I'll admit it. It's a bit embarrassing. I'm glad you asked me to stay with you, but I never thought about how we'd act the next morning. Any regrets?"

She laughed before responding.

"Regret it? No, and to make you feel better, I was thinking the same thing while you were in the bathroom. I'm glad I woke up first. I assume that finding me awake was easier on me than it was on you. No regrets at all. That said, what do we do now?"

"Awkward, yes. How about I go back to my room and take a shower? I imagine you'll want to do the same. By the time we're done, they'll be serving breakfast. I'm hungry—how about you?"

"Perfect, I am too. Call me when you're ready to go down."

CHAPTER THIRTEEN

Back in his room, Raymond kept smiling as he thought about last night.

I don't know what I expected, but it certainly isn't how the last twenty-four hours have unfolded. I'll give her this much: she's upfront about what she's thinking and what she wants. I'm glad; we only have so much time together.

Raymond showered and dressed, delaying calling Shelly, believing she would need more time to get ready than he did. He read *The Straits Times* newspaper that had been slid under his door when he returned to his room. Mostly local news, it reminded him of the *Stars and Stripes* paper he occasionally read in Vietnam.

Not much different. This paper talks about life here in Singapore, while Stars and Stripes *is about how many VC and NVA we supposedly killed the day before.*

Raymond glanced at his watch, wondering if Shelly was ready for breakfast. He picked up the phone and dialed her room.

"Hello," Shelly answered immediately, feeling foolish for not having said "Hello, Raymond."

Who else would be calling me?

"Hi, Shelly, it's Raymond."

"So you too?"

When he didn't respond right away, Shelly understood he didn't understand what she meant.

“I was sitting here, waiting for your call, knowing the only person who would call me at this hour would be you. And what do I do? I say ‘Hello,’ not ‘Hello, Ray or Raymond.’ And what do you do? You tell me who you are. What a pair we are!”

"That is funny, but I've enjoyed every moment with you, Shelly, even the awkward ones. We have so little time together—let's not worry about being embarrassed by what we do or say. I know I won't, not anymore. For God's sake, you saw me in my army boxer shorts!"

“I did. We've both been a couple of goofs on eggshells. I understand why, but no more. I'm glad you agreed to stay with me last night, Ray. Promise me you'll do so every night for the rest of this week.”

"After last night, if you hadn't asked, I would have asked you. Agreed. If you're ready for breakfast, I'll come to your room. Or do you need more time?"

"I'm ready, hungry too, I'll meet you at the elevator."

CHAPTER FOURTEEN

Breakfast finished, Shelly and Raymond decided to explore the shopping districts along Orchard Road. The walk was brief but uncomfortable due to the high temperature and humidity. Raymond realized this might not be what Shelly was hoping for.

"How are you doing, Shelly?"

"Fine, why do you ask?"

"I should have thought to ask before we got this far. It's very hot and humid, similar to what I experience every day in Vietnam. I'm so used to it, it didn't occur to me that you might not be."

"Oh, believe me, we have humidity during the wet season in Harare. I can handle it. But at some point, let's stop for something cold to drink."

"We're in the heart of what the hotel concierge called Historic Singapore. She suggested we visit the Tivoli Coffee House. I'm sure we can find something cold to drink there."

"Sounds good, lead the way."

Once inside Tivoli Gardens, they encountered a variety of restaurants, shops, rides, and attractions—much more than they had expected. And, as the hotel concierge had promised, the Tivoli Coffee House was a good place to rest after the forty-five-minute walk there. They decided to sit outside in the shade to watch people while enjoying their cold, sparkling waters.

“The concierge also recommended visiting Changi Beach, a popular spot for swimming and picnicking. She said the hotel restaurant would prepare sandwiches for us if we wanted to go. I don't have any shorts, but I can get a pair. What do you think?”

“I don't have beach clothes either, but a picnic lunch at the beach sounds fun. I do that quite often at the Harare Botanical Gardens. Yes, let's go there tomorrow. We can find something more comfortable to wear somewhere here along Orchard Road.”

Shelly and Raymond spent the rest of the day exploring the area, including buying clothes for their trip to Changi Beach the next day. Late in the afternoon, they decided to take a taxi back to the hotel to shower and rest before dinner. Raymond thought Shelly would enjoy dinner at one of the hotel restaurants. However, after looking at the prices, he decided to go out.

"I hope I didn't wear you out in the heat and humidity."

“Not at all, I enjoyed it, and I’ll be ready for more after my shower. What time do you want to go?”

“How about we meet in the lobby at six?”

"Perfect, see you at six," Shelly said as they walked to the elevator.

"You clean up nice. Did you nap?" Raymond said, watching Shelly approach him in the lobby.

"I didn't intend to, but my body overruled my mind after our day in the heat and humidity. And I'm still a little jet-lagged. I slept for an hour. I'm refreshed. What do you suggest for dinner?"

"The concierge suggested a place nearby for what's called hawker food. A blend of cultures, mostly prepared by street vendors. If that works for you, we'll take a taxi there and back. It's still warm outside, a little cooler now that the sun has set. Or we can eat here at one of the hotel restaurants if you'd rather not go out."

“Hawker food sounds interesting. I've had wonderful meals made by street vendors at home.”

"Taxis are out front. Let's go."

It took less than five minutes to reach Lau Pa Sat, where they discovered numerous food vendors offering a variety of dishes. The mingling aromas of different foods, along with the slightly cooler temperature, made Lau Pa Sat the ideal spot for dinner.

"Can you believe this? How will we ever decide what and where to eat?" Ray said, looking at all their dinner options.

"It is overwhelming, but in a good way. Why don't we each pick two or three different things we can share?"

"Sounds good. That one across the way cooking over an open hibachi looks interesting. I'll check it out," Ray said.

After making their selections, they found a table under a tree to eat and watch people as they enjoyed their dinners.

"I'm really glad we came here, Ray. I hope you are too."

"I am. The food is so good and it's not too hot out tonight. Hopefully tomorrow's picnic at the beach will go as well as tonight."

"I'm looking forward to that, too. Zimbabwe is landlocked and has no beaches. Lakes, but no easy access to an ocean. The closest one is over 800 kilometers away, through Mozambique. A day at the beach tomorrow will be wonderful."

Dinner finished, they spent another hour walking through Lau Pa Sat, taking in the sights of people enjoying themselves outside. Families with young children, couples like themselves, and older people. Everyone looked content and happy.

"What do you think? Time to head back to the hotel?" Ray asked.

"I suppose so. It is so nice out, but we have a big day ahead of us tomorrow."

Back at the hotel, before heading upstairs, Raymond talked with the concierge about planning their picnic for the next day, while Shelly went to her room to shower. The concierge said their lunch would be ready when they came down for breakfast. After that, Ray went upstairs to his room to shower before joining Shelly in her room for the night.

CHAPTER FIFTEEN

THE NEXT MORNING, RAY WOKE UP BEFORE SHELLY AND, CHECKING HIS watch, saw it was seven-thirty. He wanted to get up quietly so she could sleep a little longer, but his movement woke her.

"Good morning," she said, stretching her arms above her head. "How did you sleep?"

"Like a baby. How about you?"

"Really well. If I dreamed, I don't remember any of it."

Raymond finished getting dressed.

"I'll go back to my room to shower. Breakfast in about an hour. I'll head down a little earlier to make sure our picnic lunch order will be ready."

"Sounds good. I'll meet you downstairs."

Shelly entered the restaurant and saw Raymond sitting at a table drinking coffee.

"Do they have our picnic lunch?"

Ray reached down beside his chair and held up a bag with the sandwiches.

"Now all we need is the beach."

"I'm really excited! I looked forward to us being together here in

Singapore, but it never occurred to me that the trip would include a day at the beach. Something I would never be able to do at home."

"You will be here, but let's first have a great breakfast. Lots of options at the buffet. Are you ready?"

"Famished. Let's go."

Back at their table, they talked excitedly throughout breakfast about the day ahead.

"Waiting for you this morning, I was thinking about our time together. Everything has worked out perfectly! But then I realized, over half the week has passed. Two days from now, you go home to Zimbabwe, and I head back to the war."

Shelly put down her fork, looking off to the side in the distance.

"I hadn't thought about that. I knew the week would end, but it's going by too quickly. Now I'm sad."

"I am, too, but think of it this way: all of this was a very long shot. Asking you to meet me here, a complete stranger you only knew through a few letters. And if you agreed to come, there were no guarantees we'd get along. Shelly, I don't know how you feel, but I want you to know what I think. This week marks the start of something special for both of us."

Listening to Raymond, Shelly felt a single tear roll down her cheek. She reached for her napkin to wipe it away.

"I'm so glad to hear you say that, Raymond. I hoped you would feel something like that. I do too."

"Well, we have two days left, today at the beach. No time to be sad; let's save that for when we are flying in opposite directions. Be happy that we met, we like each other, and will plan the next time and place to be together."

"You're right. I don't know when or where that will be, but I'm already looking forward to it."

The taxi to Changi Beach took half an hour, giving Shelly and Raymond a chance to see a part of Singapore they hadn't visited before, with a temperature about ten degrees cooler than around

Orchard Road. They were happy to be here, even more so when they learned they could take the ferry to Pulau Ubin Island, just fifteen minutes from Changi Beach. Less crowded, with trails to hike and spots for picnics. A wonderful break from busy downtown Singapore.

"Shelly, this is great! We can hike, ride bikes —you do ride a bike, don't you?" Ray said.

"Actually, I don't, or maybe I should say I don't know, having never done so. Is it difficult?"

"Not once you've learned how to do it, but there is a learning curve. How about renting a two-person kayak, having our lunch somewhere away from everyone else?"

"Sitting while you paddle me to wherever that will be, sure, I can do that," Shelly said, winking at Ray.

The kayak rental agent gave them instructions in English neither of them could understand. But they nodded as though they did, signed the release form, and were soon on their way.

It didn't take long for both to realize they wouldn't get very far. They assumed being on the water would be cooler than being on land, but that turned out not to be true. The sun was relentless, made worse by reflection off the water. They spotted a shady cove, paddled over, and found a grassy spot to set up their picnic. However, a new problem quickly arose: relentless swarming mosquitoes. Back in the kayak, they paddled around, searching for a different place to have lunch.

“I see some people off to our left; their kayak is beached. They're up a bit up from the water, and the area around them doesn't look as jungle-like as where we were. Let's try that," Ray said, and he started paddling without waiting for Shelly's response.

Once there, about fifty yards from the others, they beached their kayak, walked up from the water, and found a spot to picnic, first checking for mosquitoes.

"This isn't bad, a few flying around, but much better than the other place," Shelly said, swatting at one that landed on her arm. "Let's stay here."

Relaxing in the warm sand, enjoying their sandwiches and water the restaurant packed for them, the subject of their departure came up once again.

"You're suddenly quiet. Is something bothering you?"

Hearing Raymond's question, Shelly's eyes shifted downward to the sand.

"Shelly?"

"Yes. I shouldn't, but I can't stop thinking about us separating so soon after finding each other. And worse, knowing you'll go back to the war."

Saying these last words, she broke down crying.

Raymond moved closer, putting his arm around her.

"I know, I'm feeling it too, but after this short time together, I believe we have a bright future ahead. I will get through the war. I know it scares you; it scared me at first. However, like most guys I've been with, I've learned to survive. I will, Shelly. Be sad that we have to leave soon, but don't worry about the war. We will write each other. I believe this is the start of our relationship, not the end. We have a lot to talk about regarding how and where we will be together in the future. Right now, you don't have answers to those questions. I don't either. But soon, we will. Trust me."

Hearing this made Shelly feel a little better. Not completely, especially not about Raymond going back to the war. Just a better now, closer to the end of their week together.

CHAPTER SIXTEEN

RAYMOND, NOW YOU UNDERSTAND WHAT SHELLY'S TIME ALONE IN Singapore was like, not knowing why you weren't there with her, fearing the worst. And both of you know what that time might have been like if you had been together.

You parted, reassuring each other and yourselves that you would keep your relationship alive through letters. You were killed, Raymond, and that never happened. However, you both can imagine what those letters would have said if you hadn't died in the war.

Shelly and Raymond considered what this meant, not just about the letters but about their relationship as a couple. Did either of them want to pursue a relationship with so many challenges? How could letters that were never written reveal what they needed to know?

Having come this far, they knew there was no alternative to learning what would have been.

CHAPTER SEVENTEEN

Dear Shelly,

Leaving you, seeing you crying at the gate as I boarded my plane, was one of the hardest things I've ever had to do. I wanted to turn around and comfort you, telling you everything will work out for both of us. Obviously, I couldn't do that. Before our time together in Singapore, I pictured myself flying back to the war, focused on what awaited me. That didn't happen; instead, all I could think about was you crying. I've been back for two weeks now. The same old grind as before my R&R, but it's easier now, remembering us together in Singapore. I will be fine, Shelly—please believe me. I hope you are as well.

Dear Raymond,

Watching you walk to your plane was horrible, but I feel so bad knowing I made it harder for you. I'm better now, back to my 'grind,' missing you terribly. I'm doing my best to accept what must be, still afraid because I don't know what that is or will become. Not just knowing that you are in danger every single day you are there. There's something more I hesitate to tell you. Please don't think I'm crazy. Something strange has been happening since I returned to Harare.

A young woman's voice speaks to me clearly. She says her name is Eden Quinn. She says you are her father, and I am her mother. She says she is lost because we now believe we are living our immortal lives. I am not making this up. It's all so real, it scares me.

Dear Shelly,

How do I begin?

Even before we were together in Singapore, I occasionally dreamed what my life would be like once I was out of the army. I would go back to school and graduate from college. I would get a good job, get married, have children—all the things most everyone in my platoon dreams about, one way or another. Being with you in Singapore, I told myself that while I don't know which college I will attend, what I will study, what job I will have, or where I will live, I now know who my wife will be. You, Shelly. My dreams about the future now include you—not just some unknown person I hope to meet, fall in love with, and marry someday.

I might have mentioned some of that to you in a letter before we were together, or maybe while we were in Singapore. I don't remember doing so, but based on what you've written, it's possible, or I could have talked in my sleep.

I hope to become a father, and if I have a daughter, I would like to use my mother's middle name as her middle name. Shelly, that name is Eden. I must have mentioned it to you in a letter, or while we were together in Singapore, whether awake or asleep. Eden is a family name that has been passed down through my family for generations. It is not common, and there is no other explanation for you hearing it other than it coming from me.

Dear Raymond,

I have read and reread your latest letter countless times. I have tried to remember everything we discussed while we were together. I have your letters from before your R&R. There is no mention of naming your children, nothing about one you would name Eden. I don't recall you saying anything about naming your children. I don't remember you talking in your sleep. This young woman's voice, telling me we are her parents, that she is lost, and that her name is Eden, only began after I returned to Harare from Singapore.

CHAPTER EIGHTEEN

Come to Other Worlds. I will help you.

Shelly and Raymond sat in overstuffed leather chairs, each flanking Asian, with coffee on small tables between them. No windows, doors, or Vietnam posters on the walls. No barista at the bar, or other customers sitting nearby. They sat in silence, neither speaking nor thinking about anything except what might soon happen.

"My name is Đoàn ăn Giáp. Raymond, you referred to me as Asian. To you, Shelly, I was your conscience until recently, when I told both of you that, regardless of who or what you think I am, I am here to guide you both to your immortal existence. I requested that you be here together to discuss your journeys to immortality. Please settle your minds. I have answers for questions you haven't known to ask. Answers that will help you learn what you must now do."

"You both are questioning what each has to do with the other. You recall meeting at Starbucks. You would have met here the next day as well. Shelly, you left before Raymond arrived. You asked me to tell him he had something that belonged to you, something you wanted him to have. Raymond, you thought you knew what that was, and when you couldn't find it, you assumed you had dreamed all of it. Dreams play a very special role in both our mortal and immortal lives. In my mortal life, which ended forty-six years ago, in yours, Raymond, and ever since in the search for our immortal selves. I will guide you both, as I have many others who have experienced what you are now experiencing. I am like you both, with one big difference. I know answers to questions you do not."

Neither Shelly nor Raymond spoke. They just sat, waiting for Asian to continue.

"You have heard the letters you would have written to each other after your time together in Singapore over forty-six years ago. An unlived life had you not been killed in action, Raymond." Giáp paused briefly before continuing, "Had I not killed you. In one sense, you have both been dead a long time. In another, you have searched ever since for your immortal existence, encountering each other in numerous places and situations, unaware of the connection between you. However, as of this moment, you both now clearly recall everything that has happened to each of you separately and together in the forty-six years since you died, Raymond, the forty-one years since you died, Shelly."

Hearing this, Raymond and Shelly looked directly at each other, their shocked expressions softening into gratitude. After so many years in so many places, they finally recognized the connection between them.

Raymond stood up and moved toward Shelly, who was now standing as well. They embraced, both silently thinking, *"This is what we've been searching for; we are together forever." We no longer have questions.*

"You have answers for the questions you knew to ask, but not for those you didn't. I didn't bring you here so that you could learn what you already know. There is more for you to consider. In a way, you are living what you both hope would be your immortal lives. Together, not knowing any more than what you do, happy with only that much. But that is not your immortality; you are only acting as though it were, and that has created a new problem in the multiverse. You believe you have found what you would like your immortality to be, but that was never for you to decide, based on knowing so little."

Raymond responded. "More for us to learn? What more could there be? We have found each other, and that's all we've ever wanted. Why isn't that enough?"

"What does the two of you having 'found' yourselves together mean for so many others?"

"What do you mean, others?"

Raymond and Shelly quietly returned to their seats as though compelled to do so.

"Raymond, you have said you want to be married and have children. You visited some of your unlived lives with women, one of whom you married and had children with. Shelly, you were in relationships with other men, married at one point, living with another, and had a baby. What happens to those souls? What happens to the children the two of you know you had in some of your unlived lives? What about those you would have later, the ones you haven't met in an unlived life? What happens to Eden? Why is she reaching out to you, Shelly, her mother, and you, Raymond, her father? You didn't dream Eden into Shelly's consciousness, Raymond. You didn't mumble about her in your sleep. She's reaching out to both of you now because, you believe, with little basis for doing so, that you have found your immortal lives. Because you have, without justification, your daughter from a different, unlived life is prevented from living hers."

Shelly sat in her chair, her head tilted down, avoiding eye contact with Giáp and Raymond. Raymond turned toward Giáp, quickly standing up, looking for a different place to be in Other Worlds. There was nowhere to go, only blank walls, and no furniture except the chairs occupied by Giáp, Shelly, and himself. He sat back down.

"What do we do, Giáp?" Raymond said, looking in Shelly's direction.

Giáp did not respond; instead, thinking thoughts that both Shelly and Raymond heard.

You know what you must do.

CHAPTER NINETEEN

Her easel set up on the sidewalk with no one passing by, Eden Quinn looked around, wondering why she had decided this was where she would sketch a gritty portrait of Seattle that few would ever see. Plenty of other rough locations with their own fallen human 'leaves' blowing across the concrete also existed. Gray clouds overhead threatened rain that could fall on whatever she drew. Why here? She only knew it had to be this city, this place, with whatever people and situations she might encounter.

She began the drawing with words on a sign above a building she could not see. Adjacent to a viaduct covering a fenced-off area below, much of which was filled with random trash, she chalked "Other Worlds."

"Interesting!"

Eden turned to see an Asian man standing directly behind her. She had not heard him approach.

Where did he come from?

"It looks like a sign. Add 'Coffee' on the end, and it would be."

"I don't know why I came up with that, but it has nothing to do with coffee."

The Asian man laughed. "Are you sure? You're standing less than twenty feet from the entrance to Other Worlds Coffee," he said, pointing over her shoulder under the viaduct.

Eden turned to look in the direction she had been facing when the man approached from behind her.

How could I miss that? What happened to the fence? It was here, I'm sure of it, but it's not now.

"My name's Giáp. I haven't seen you around here before. Add a little more shading for depth, and you'll create a good representation of the Other Worlds Coffee sign."

"Thanks, I'm Eden. I've not been here before, and I'm not sure why I am now. I thought the area and overcast sky lighting would be good for a black-and-white chalk drawing. Once here, I didn't find much to draw until you came along and pointed out what I completely missed. Where *did* you come from? I missed seeing you, too."

"Just here for a quick coffee, and since it's cold and you're only drawing that sign, come on in to warm up. My treat: coffee, tea, whatever you like. Welcome to Other Worlds!" he said, expecting Eden to follow. She gathered her easel, putting her paper, chalk, and pencils in her art shoulder bag, and followed him to the front door.

As she entered, she immediately felt she'd been here before, knowing she hadn't. A case of inexplicable déjà vu. The room was comfortably warm, the scent of leather drifting from the half dozen chairs scattered around. A few patrons sitting near her, their drinks beside them, engaging in quiet conversations that Eden couldn't hear. She was glad to be here.

"Here's your coffee, Eden. Be careful, it's very hot."

She accepted it, sitting in the leather chair next to the one Giáp sat in.

"If you want to draw, how about something inside since you didn't find much outside? I checked with the barista. He said that would be fine, but don't look too obvious while observing others. They might not like being drawn. Aside from those two, friends of mine. Ask first, but I bet they'll say it's okay." He pointed to a middle-aged couple sitting nearby.

Eden looked around and in the couple's direction. "I did come a long way only to write, not draw, two words," she said, smiling at Giáp. "If you think they won't mind."

Giáp replied, "Let's find out. Follow me."

Eden followed him over to the couple.

"Shelly, Raymond, this is Eden, an artist I met out front, wondering what to draw. She'd like to do an interior scene. Would either of you mind if she included the two of you sitting with your backs to her, doing just what you're doing now, relaxing with your coffee?"

Eden wondered how he could have described the scene she pictured so precisely.

Raymond replied, "I'm fine with it. Shelly?"

"Sure, why not? Happy to meet you, Eden," Shelly said, holding out her hand for Eden to shake.

"Thank you, Shelly, you too, Raymond."

"You're welcome. Are you from around here?"

"No," she said, stepping a few feet back from the chairs Raymond and Shelly were sitting in, to set up her easel and prepare her drawing supplies.

"I'll leave the three of you to handle it from here," Giáp said, heading for the door. "I need to step outside to return a call. Do a good job, Eden. I look forward to seeing your work."

"I'll try, but reserve judgment until you see more than just the two words you saw outside," Eden said, as she began the first strokes of her initial Other Worlds portrait.

It would not be her last.

CHAPTER TWENTY

SHE DOESN'T KNOW WHO WE ARE, RAYMOND.

I know, but since she's in Seattle, she must know something about me. It's too much of a coincidence for her not to.

Giáp said we believed we had found and were living our immortal lives. Because of that, we are preventing Eden from living her mortal life and discovering her eternal existence. What does that mean?

"You denied Eden a mortal life when you were killed, Raymond. Not intentionally, but everything that would have become your mortal future ended that day. Shelly, you killed yourself believing you could no longer tolerate the pain you suffered, not knowing what happened to Raymond. The decisions both of you made led to your mortal deaths. Eden was never born, and, like you, her soul is now searching for her immortal existence—one she will never find without your help. You both must find yours as well. You haven't thought about those who will never live as mortals. There would only have been one; her name would have been Eden. Her unborn soul called out to you, Shelly; the mother she never knew. All souls exist before mortal birth, and after the mortal body they inhabit ceases to exist. Until you resolve your immortality, Eden's soul will be trapped between the mortal life she never lived and her immortal existence. Eden is lost in the multiverse."

Will she ever acknowledge Shelly or me? How can she know Shelly would have been her mother, me her father?

"Newborn animals immediately recognize their parents. Can you not imagine humans doing the same? If so, consider the situation from a different perspective. Shelly said a young woman's voice called out to her, asking for help. She said she is lost. You have no explanation for how that could have happened. You are living as if you have found your immortal existence, the only one possible for the two of you. You haven't, and unless you do what you can to resolve this issue, Eden's soul will be condemned to search for her immortality alone, never finding it. Are you willing to accept that consequence, not only for yourselves but also for the young girl who would have been your daughter had you both lived?"

No, we do not. What do we do?

"Begin by accepting that Eden is now in Other Worlds for the same reasons you both have been and are again now. Raymond, you accepted that realizing your mortal life ended forty-six years ago helped you understand that you are caught between that long-ago mortal life and the immortality you seek. Shelly, you are as well. Both of you, lost souls searching for the only future possible, one that includes Eden. Never tell her about your past; she wouldn't believe you. You are not there to tell her what she must do, only to help her find her own way. Restart your searches for immortality, freeing Eden to begin hers. I will help all three of you."

CHAPTER TWENTY-ONE

"ALMOST FINISHED? WE'RE EAGER TO SEE WHAT YOU'VE DRAWN."

Eden paused before responding, looking intently at the completed drawing on her easel. A drawing she had no recollection of making, the scene not from the back of the couple sitting in their chairs. Instead, they faced forward, smiling, looking comfortable.

"You want to see it now?" Eden asked, still staring at the drawing, completely confused how it came to be.

"Yes, Eden, can we see it?" Shelly stood up and walked toward Eden and the drawing, waiting for permission to look at it.

Eden looked at Shelly and Raymond, both now standing, confused by what she saw. In the drawing, they were facing her and her easel, while they should be facing the other way with their backs to her. The drawing was nothing as she intended. Shelly's and Raymond's faces looked incredibly lifelike—too much so for her to have drawn, especially since she had only seen them briefly before starting.

Eden stumbled in her reply, first looking at Shelly and Raymond, and down again at the drawing.

"I...I don't know what to say. I thought you were okay with me drawing you from behind. I thought that's what I did. The last I recall, you were both sitting in those chairs facing away from me. Now the chairs are turned around. I just saw you both get up from them, facing me, and...," she again stared at the drawing. "This drawing, it's on my paper, my easel, created by my pencils and chalk. But I don't recognize it. I don't see how I could have drawn either of you so accurately."

"Shelly and I watched you for the last half hour. We mentioned something about you drawing us from behind. I don't remember when or how that changed, but it definitely did. Can we see it? I'm sure you did a great job."

Still confused, Raymond's suggested explanation being the only one she could imagine, she turned the easel around to face them. "Yes, maybe seeing it will tell the three of us how this happened. I can't explain it."

"Oh my gosh, Eden, you are such a talent. I've never cared much for caricatures. I thought that might be what you would draw. This is unbelievable. It's like you took a photograph of Raymond and me."

"Incredibly lifelike, Eden; wonderful work. You are very talented," Giáp said, without anyone noticing or commenting when he entered the room. "Have you been formally trained as an artist, or does this come naturally to you? We didn't discuss your background outside, or when we came in, before I stepped out for my call. But seeing this, I'd like to know more about you."

Two more chairs appeared near Shelly's and Raymond's, along with a small table for their drinks. No one questioned it; it was all just there when needed.

"Please, everyone, have a seat. I'd like to hear more about you, Eden, and I bet Shelly and Raymond would too."

Eden felt uneasy about everything: how everyone thought her drawing was so realistic, and why it was facing a different way than she had planned. And now, Giáp was showing interest in learning more about her.

"I don't know. I mean, what would you like to know?"

Raymond spoke first.

"I grew up not far from here. Are you from Seattle or the nearby area? There are many artists in Seattle; it's clear you are one of them."

Still occasionally glancing over her shoulder at the drawing she didn't remember creating, Eden quietly said, "Not from here, but close enough. I haven't had formal training; I just gravitated toward art. It's something I could do reasonably well."

"More than reasonably well, Eden, much more," Shelly said. "So you are not from here. Where will you go next?"

Eden looked back at the three of them looking at her.

"A good question I often ask myself. I don't know. I am searching for a place I will know I should be. I haven't found it yet."

"Can you see yourself giving Seattle or somewhere nearby a chance, or is this the only one you will do?" Giáp asked.

"Another good question. I need to make money. I thought I might do that by drawing for tourists along the waterfront. You met me here because I wanted to try without the crowds before being among them. You've all encouraged me with your response," she said, again looking back at the drawing, "but I'd like to try some more to make sure whatever happened here wasn't a fluke.

Giáp responded without waiting for Shelly or Raymond to speak.

"You lack self-confidence, Eden. It's helpful to recognize your strengths and weaknesses, but you also need to be ready to assert yourself to achieve your goals. It appears you don't clearly know what those goals are. It sounds like you're just looking for a way to make money. If you don't mind, I have a suggestion. Instead of us asking what you want to do, why not draw a picture of what you want to accomplish? If we can see what you have in mind and describe it to you, you'd be ready to compete with the best artists along the waterfront and beyond. What do you think?"

Eden didn't answer, causing Giáp to explain more.

"To be clearer, I mean what you are searching for—what you hope to find. That could be a place, a person, a situation, or possibly all three."

"I need to think more about what I should draw. I think you're suggesting I am being too vague. Maybe being more specific would help? Can we talk about this more later?"

"Certainly. Is there anything else I can help you with now?" Giáp said.

"No, but I do have a question for you, Shelly and Raymond," she said, turning toward them.

Shelly replied, "Absolutely, ask anything you like, Eden."

"Why are you here?"

Shelly and Raymond looked at each other as though deciding who would respond. Raymond spoke first.

"Do you mean here in Other Worlds, Seattle, or somewhere else?"

“Another good question for which I don't have an answer. I don't know. Initially, coffee, I suppose, but then you were both willing to sit while I drew you, a drawing I don't recall doing. And now I look around, and I don't see any other people here as there were when I first walked in with you, Giáp. I haven't seen anyone come in or leave, just the four of us. I recall you saying you had to step outside to make a call, but I didn't see you leave or return. So much about today feels strange.”

Giáp responded.

“Very observant of you, Eden. It is a strange place compared to all other Seattle coffee shops. That's why I am here, and I believe why Raymond and Shelly are as well," he turned toward them, both nodding in agreement. "But I have some things to take care of the rest of the afternoon. Can we agree to meet here again tomorrow morning? Shelly, Raymond, would you join us?"

Shelly leaned toward Eden, speaking almost in a whisper.

"Strange doesn't begin to describe this place and what happens here. Good to hear I'm not the only one who thinks so.”

Shelly turned toward Giáp. “Yes, we will be here, as we are most days; you never disappoint us."

“Thank you, Shelly, you too, Raymond. I try, and if 'strange' is all you ever call me, I accept.”

Standing up, he continued, "Okay, ten tomorrow. I'm buying, including breakfast rolls for those who sleep in, skipping breakfast."

CHAPTER TWENTY-TWO

"I'M GLAD YOU MADE IT, EDEN. WHAT WOULD YOU LIKE TO DRINK? HOT or cold tea, maybe orange juice or water? Something to eat? I expect Shelly and Raymond will be here shortly."

"Black coffee would be fine, nothing to eat, thank you. Can I ask you something?"

"Sure, anything you'd like."

"Raymond and Shelly aren't just random coffee shop customers, are they?"

"Why do you ask?"

"I couldn't get them and my drawing of them out of my mind last night. It has something to do with them and me. I don't know what it is, but I am sure there is a connection."

Giáp preferred this not to come up first thing this morning. He knew it would eventually, but he wanted to address it when he felt the time was right.

"You are correct, to a point, but there is much more to it than you know. Trust me, Eden, you will understand in time."

"Sorry, we're late, no excuse. What were you saying about coffee and breakfast rolls, Giáp?"

"One or both, whichever you prefer, Raymond."

"A roll with water, thank you."

"A roll and coffee for me, Giáp. Good morning, Eden. Did you sleep well?" Shelly said, sitting down next to Eden.

"I suppose so, I'm never really sure. I often wake up thinking I remembered something I had to do, only to realize it was just a dream. There isn't a clear line between my world awake and asleep; one overlaps the other."

"I understand. It's usually the bad dreams that take time to realize were just dreams."

"Thank you, Giáp," Shelly said, accepting the breakfast roll and coffee he placed in front of her, doing the same for Raymond and Eden.

"My pleasure. While you eat, let me share my thoughts after we finished yesterday. That might help us understand each other better this morning. I thought I could skillfully guide you to a conclusion we all agree on by the end of today. Maybe I could, but your question, Eden, before Shelly and Raymond arrived this morning, tells me it is better to skip the 'steering' and get straight to the point. Eden said she did not believe the two of you were random coffee customers, particularly after the sudden appearance of what she is still not convinced is her drawing."

He turned to Eden before continuing.

"Yesterday, I said you are very observant. I'll say it again this morning. Eden, you truly are, and you deserve to be recognized for it. From now on, everything I tell you will be the plain truth. Shelly and Raymond are not random coffee customers. They were here yesterday, and they are here now to help you understand your life. I will share more about that later this morning, but for now, I'd like to give you some additional information. So far, so good?"

Eden looked at Giáp, Raymond, and Shelly separately as though one of them would tell the truth, and the other two would not.

"Yes, that is more of a response to my question than I expected. Thank you."

"Good, I will only say what I am about to because I believe you can handle it. I doubt I could have 'steered' you very far anyway. Eden, you are the first and only person to enter Other Worlds Coffee whose mortal life has not ended. You were right to say this place is strange; it would be to any mortal still alive. However, you are not, and never have been mortal. You were never born into mortal life. You weren't," he said, looking first at Raymond, then quickly at Shelly, "because Raymond died forty-six years ago, and Shelly five years after him. You called out to Shelly for help without knowing you did. She only knew you to be a young woman by the sound of your voice. The souls of most people who die immediately transition to an immortal existence. That didn't happen for Raymond and Shelly, and they are now searching for their immortal lives. And although you've never been mortal, you are searching for yours as well. They can help you in your search, Eden. I can too. You do not have to accept that help. If you choose not to, all this will be erased from your memory, and you will return to the life you knew before hearing this today, lost in the multiverse. But you must first learn more about them before deciding what to do."

"Raymond and Shelly both led mortal lives. He was a US soldier serving in the Vietnam War. He and Shelly, who at the time lived in Zimbabwe, were communicating through letters. He was killed in the war, with no word from anyone telling Shelly what happened to him. She became distraught and ultimately took her own life five years after Raymond's death. One of the lives they could have lived had they made different choices would have been to marry and have only one child. That child would have been you, Eden."

CHAPTER TWENTY-THREE

Raymond and Shelly were stunned to hear Giáp reveal so much to Eden so quickly. They sat silently, Raymond leaning forward in his chair, head bowed, arms resting on his knees, his hands clasped in front of him as if praying. Shelly leaned back, resting her head on the chair's back, head tilted up, eyes closed, with a pained expression on her face as if she were about to cry. Eden's eyes were wide open, looking back and forth at them and Giáp, trying to make sense of his explanation. However, this was not entirely a surprise to her. She knew something in her life was not right. She felt she lived more in her dreams than when she was awake.

What do I do with what Giáp just said?

"That is the right question, Eden, but don't try to answer just yet. Unless you tell me you have no interest in exploring this further, I have a suggestion. Something that will help you decide what to do."

Eden looked to Giáp, her voice no louder than a whisper.

"What is it?"

"Yesterday, I suggested you draw what you want to achieve instead of explaining it to us. You thought I was talking about your art. Not exactly, but I hoped that whatever you drew would help you understand what is ahead for you. I didn't intend to explain everything so quickly. I did this morning because you asked specific questions I needed to answer. My goal, then and now, is for you to share what's in your mind and heart through drawing, rather than verbally describing your thoughts. Will you do that?"

Eden looked back at Raymond and Shelly, both still unable to look at her directly.

"And what will happen if that produces nothing to help the three of you or me?"

"You are not here to help us, Eden; we are here to help you. If nothing changes for you, you won't be any worse off than you are now. You can choose to return to the life you knew before our time together, or decide to continue with us in search of resolution."

Eden stood up and walked away from Giáp, Shelly, and Raymond, as if looking for a place to be alone. She turned back toward them, her eyes fixed on her easel and art supplies bag.

"I will try to draw what I cannot describe to the three of you. There's nothing more I can do."

Shelly and Raymond sat upright, pleased but still anxious about what might happen next. Giáp spoke.

"I understand how upsetting this is for you, Eden. I wish there were another way to help you. Unfortunately, there isn't. This is the only option available to you. I hope that what you draw will help us understand you better. If it does, we will be able to help you more. If it doesn't, you will be no worse off than you are now."

Eden set up her easel, took out her pencils, chalk, and paper from her bag. Before starting, she faced Giáp, Shelly, and Raymond one last time. They were no longer in the room. She turned back to the easel and began to draw.

CHAPTER TWENTY-FOUR

HER DRAWING WAS COMPLETE, STILL ATTACHED TO THE EASEL PAD, covered by a single sheet of blank paper. Eden put her supplies back in her bag and turned toward Giáp, Shelly, and Raymond, now seated facing her.

"Before I show you my drawing, I want to share what it means to me. Thank you, Giáp, for encouraging me to do this. I was surprised how quickly it came together, and I'm very pleased with what I believe it reveals. It brings clarity to my situation. We will now see what, if anything, it does for the three of you."

Eden turned the easel to face them, lifting the blank page from her drawing to reveal an image of a healthy tree floating above a vast chasm, as if it might fall and be swallowed by the Earth. Looking back at her drawing, she ran her index finger from the tree canopy down to where the roots would be.

"Roots do not anchor this tree, and because they don't, it shouldn't even exist. If it falls, it will be swallowed by the Earth, lost forever. You say I was never born because the two people who would have been my parents" —she paused, looking at Shelly and Raymond—"died before conceiving me. And yet, they are here with me now. That comforts me. I believe they, and you, Giáp, may be able to help me. But help me do what I do not understand."

Giáp paused before responding, looking at Shelly, noticing tears in her eyes.

"Your interpretation of your drawing reveals more about you than you realize, Eden. You are 'lost' without ever having been born. You have been searching and calling out to someone you didn't know—the one person who would have been your mother. You couldn't have known what all this means. The three of you have much to learn about yourselves and each other as you experience echoes of Eden's unlived lives. Raymond and Shelly, you have 'roots' for your mortal lives. Eden did not, but she does now. Eden, cling to them and me—the only three souls in the entire metaverse who can help you find your eternal forever. You are no longer alone."

Looking at all three of them, Giáp continued.

"It is time for you to resume your individual and collective searches, this time as the family you would have been had you made different choices in the past."

Like the calm after a storm, Eden, Shelly, and Raymond feel a new beginning for all three of them.

CHAPTER TWENTY-FIVE

Eden's life in Gràcia, Barcelona, was generally good, especially after she met Agustín six months earlier. Until then, her days involved creating chalk-and-pencil drawings for tourists in Gràcia and spending time with friends for wine and food at tapas bars near their apartments. Warm summer nights, the smells of these places blended with marijuana, like cloth draped over the street and everyone in it. Exactly the bohemian life she'd hoped to find. But something was missing, and she believed she had found it in Agustín, an aspiring poet and photographer.

"Eden, let me take another picture of you. I don't have enough."

Focused on her drawing, Eden answered, trying to sound a little irritated while feeling happy he was with her this late July night in her flat.

"Not now, or anytime soon, Agustín! You have enough of me. Let me finish my drawing. If I don't, I'll have nothing to sell, and then who will pay for your wine and tapas?" she said, continuing to draw from memory the Plaça de John Lennon favored by tourists visiting Gràcia.

While fairly content with her life, Eden wondered if this was where and how she would spend the rest of her days. Making pencil drawings for tourists, spending time with Agustín, and a few close friends living nearby who seemed to her to have no more direction than she did. But there was a difference between them and her. They didn't ask themselves such questions.

She could barely remember much of her early life before moving to Spain. It felt as if her life only truly began *after* she arrived in Spain on a warm summer night breeze. She enjoyed imagining what her destiny might be.

Will I still be doing this ten, twenty, or thirty years from now? Will I have children, whether or not I am married? Agustín doesn't worry about these things, but I do.

But there was more bothering her than just her future. Eden felt lost in the world around her. Everyone else seemed to know exactly where they were, where they were headed. Most had close ties to large families and many friends. If they worried or wondered about their future, they didn't let it show.

"Okay, Eden, if you won't let me take your picture on this beautiful night, I will go out to meet our friends for a glass of Rioja before bed. Keep working if you must," he said, wrapping his arms around her and kissing her gently on the neck.

"As you must, Agustín," she said, not responding to his embrace and never taking her eyes off her drawing. An hour later, too tired to go on, she set it aside, planning to start again in the morning after what she hoped would be a good night's sleep.

Eden, you have something to ask me. What is it?

I say I am happy, but I'm not.

Do you know why you aren't? Is it Agustín?

It's not about him personally. I am happier now that he's in my life than I was before we met. It's something much bigger than a personal relationship. With or without Agustín and my friends, I feel alone. I have no real connection to anyone.

Raymond, Giáp, and I are your connection. You are not lost. Your drawings reveal great emotional depth and resilience, far beyond what the subjects you draw deserve. Tourists buying your work might not see this; they just feel compelled to buy. You are connected to them only in that way. If you believe these feelings are for you, you can find love, acceptance, and connection in many forms. Do you, Eden?

I want to, Shelly. But I don't know.

It's okay that you don't know now. You will soon. I will help you. Raymond and Giáp will too. Sleep now.

CHAPTER TWENTY-SIX

Eden remembered last night's dream, a recurring one she'd had frequently over the past few months. It was a conversation with a woman named Shelly, married to her father, Raymond. Dreaming this made her feel better.

I dream about my family; why don't I know more about them? Where are they? Are they still alive, living somewhere, maybe wondering about me? I often asked Agustín about his family, and now he's taking me to meet his mother. Not because our relationship has grown to the point that he wants us to meet. Probably because he's just tired of me asking about her.

Agustín picked Eden up at her flat ten-thirty Sunday morning. They took a short walk to the Fontana Metro Station. Three stops later, they got off at Penitents, followed by a short walk to the neighborhood where Agustín grew up. Neither his mother nor Agustín had suggested they meet; it was only happening because Eden asked so many questions about his childhood, his mother, and his father, who had passed away unexpectedly five years earlier. They planned to have lunch together after a quick visit at his mother's apartment. Eden felt nervous.

"It's funny," Eden said once off the train. "I'm going to meet your mother, not because she asked to meet me. That would be normal; mothers would naturally want to meet a woman her son might someday marry. No, instead I wanted to meet her to see where you grew up because I don't recall much about that part of my life. I guess I want to live vicariously through you."

"Whatever your reason, it's fine with me. I hope she's home from church. She knows we're coming to take her to lunch."

They walked up the building stairs leading to his mother's third-floor apartment. Agustín tried the door, and finding it unlocked, they entered, he calling to his mother.

"Mamá, estamos aquí, ¿Dónde estás?"

"En el dormitorio, terminándome de arreglar. Salgo en un minuto."

"She's almost ready, just another minute or so."

Agustín's mother walked out shortly after, greeting and hugging her son.

"Mamá, me gustaría presentarte a mi amiga, Edén. Edén, ella es mi madre, Mila. I introduced you, and you to her. Her name is Mila."

"I am so happy to meet you, Mila," she said, turning to Agustín. "Is that her first name? Can I call her that?"

"Everyone does."

"I'm so happy to meet you, Mila. Thank you for having me at your home today."

Not bothering to translate Eden's response to his mother or suggesting they sit and talk in her apartment, Agustín instead asked if she was ready to go to lunch.

"I thought you said we would talk here for a while," Eden said.

"I did, but we can do that at lunch. And I see I have a lot of tiring translation to do regardless of where we are."

They arrived at a nearby tapas cafe and were quickly seated. The waiter took their food and drink order, and a few awkward moments of silence settled over them. Eden decided to take charge.

"Ask your mother if there is anything she would like to know about me."

"Are you sure you want me to do that? You don't know what she might ask."

"That's okay, ask her anyway."

"Mamá, Eden quiere saber si hay algo sobre ella que quieras preguntar. Dentro de lo razonable, mamá, no la avergüences ni a mí, por favor."

Turning to Eden, he said, "I asked her to be reasonable, not to embarrass me or you."

Smiling, slightly embarrassed, Mama replied, "Bueno, me preguntaba si ella quería conocerme porque ustedes dos están planeando casarse."

Hearing this, Agustín sat up straight in his chair, responding to his mother, "Ay, Dios mío, madre, te pedí que no me avergonzaras. No estamos aquí para eso; solo quería conocerte."

Eden could see that Agustín was uncomfortable, while his mother appeared pleased with herself. She insisted that he translate, and he shifted in his chair before responding.

"I told her you wondered if there was anything she wanted to ask about you, and she responded that she had thought we might be here to tell her we would soon marry. I just knew this would not go well."

Eden laughed out loud, pointing at herself and Agustín.

"I do like your son, Mama, but no, not getting married. We will see," Eden said, reaching across the table to hold Mama's hands, both of them laughing.

Lunch finished, they walked Mama back upstairs to her flat. Eden hugged her, thanking her for taking the time to spend this afternoon together. Mama responded, Agustín, translating that she had a great time as well and hoped they could soon spend more time together.

Once off the metro ride back to Fontana Station, Eden asked, "You know what the best part of meeting your mother was for me?" Eden said, trying not to laugh.

"No, but I have an idea. What was it?"

"Watching you squirm when she told you why she thought we asked to meet."

"I made a point of telling her that was *not* why we wanted to come. I asked her not to embarrass me. She knew it would and did it anyway. Oh, Dios mío, mamá."

Still laughing, Eden replied, "No es necesaria ninguna traducción."

CHAPTER TWENTY-SEVEN

DID ASKING TO MEET AGUSTÍN'S MOTHER HAVE ANYTHING TO DO WITH YOUR relationship with him?

No, it did not. Being completely honest, I've been thinking about what I've missed not being born, wondering what it feels like to have a mother. I wanted to meet his mother to see how they interacted.

Eden, I know I'm not your mother, but doesn't my wishing I had been, knowing I would have been if Raymond hadn't been killed in the war, mean something to you?

It does, and you do too, Shelly. So do you, Raymond, when you say you wish you could have been my father. The fact that you did not live to become my parents is not your fault. I now understand why I wasn't born. I feel sorry for you both—not because you missed out on raising me, but because I am forcing you to deal with it now.

You are not forcing us to do anything, Eden. Shelly, Giáp, and I are encouraging you to confront your situation. We understand that is difficult for you, just as it was for us when we had to face our own reality. We're doing this to help you, which also helps us.

I know, but I still feel a void in my life.

You are the void, Eden. Shelly, Raymond, and I are here to help you fill it. That might not happen quickly, maybe never. But keep trying. Ask questions, share your feelings. We are those connections you say you lack. One day, you will see we have been with you all along.

CHAPTER TWENTY-EIGHT

Life for Eden and Agustín went on much the same as it had since they met. Both pursued artistic careers, with Eden doing better financially than Agustín. But to Eden, he seemed happy, satisfied with their relationship and his life overall, and, for reasons she couldn't explain to herself, she did not feel the same. She had growing doubts about them as a couple, and when she was honest enough to admit it to herself, she felt uncertain about everything in her life.

When I moved to Barcelona two years ago, I envisioned the life I am living now. I am an artist among other artists, living in a bohemian neighborhood. I love my friends. But something is not right. There is a void I need to fill.

You've said that before, Eden—a void. You can't fill it if you don't understand what it is. Something is missing from your life. Raymond, Shelly, and I want to help. We believe you know what is missing, and are choosing not to acknowledge it. If you are not where you are meant to be, you must find that place. You will do that depending on which unlived lives you choose to visit. You will know when it is time to leave a place, person, or situation. Do not minimize the importance of what you choose. Do not put off changing something you know is wrong. Doing so is a decision, the consequences of which will end your ability to choose your immortal life.

CHAPTER TWENTY-NINE

EDEN AND AGUSTÍN WORKED MOST WEEKDAYS AND MANY WEEKENDS. There were plenty of opportunities for Eden to sell her drawings and for Agustín to photograph things and people to make money. Still, they made time for each other and for hanging out with friends on Wednesday nights for tapas and wine.

"How long have the two of you been together, Eden? Eva asked, while Agustín and Edwardo, Eva's boyfriend, were ordering another bottle of wine at the bar. "It seems like years,"

"Years? Hmm, it sometimes feels like that or even longer," Eden replied, staring off into the distance.

Eva decided not to press, believing Eden preferred they talk about something else, until Eden looked at her with questions of her own.

"Eva, both you and Edwardo have family nearby, don't you?"

"Not far, easy to get to both families on the metro."

"Do you see both frequently?"

"I see my mother and father at least once a month, sometimes with Edwardo, other times alone if he is busy with something else."

"If you don't mind me asking, do you visit them because you have to? An obligation because they are your parents?"

"An obligation? I don't think so. I mean, sometimes there are things I'd rather do, but I enjoy seeing my parents, and I know they enjoy seeing me." She paused before continuing, thinking about what Eden was asking. "Now that you ask, I think they like seeing Edwardo as well, and he's never said he did not want to go with me. But they are my parents, and he sometimes visits his while I'm with mine. Why all these questions about how much we see our parents?"

Eden looked away, unsure whether she would answer truthfully or try to change the subject. Eva was her friend. Eden had brought up the topic; she would answer her honestly.

"Eva, if I answer you, you have to promise you won't tell Edwardo or any of our friends what I've said. Do you promise?"

Although Eva believed their conversation had been casual so far, she could tell it had now turned serious.

"I promise. Are you okay?"

Eden looked to see if Agustín and Edwardo were about to return to the table. They were still at the bar, laughing and toasting each other with shots of some alcohol. The bottle of wine they planned to bring back sat on the bar next to them. She turned back to Eva.

"No, I am not, Eva. I am very unhappy. I asked about your families, the time you spend with them, and whether you do so out of obligation. Part of me wished you would say you'd rather spend the time doing other things. I know that's horrible of me, but I'm telling you the truth. I did so because—," she paused to gather in her emotions. "I did so because I envy you and Edwardo, Agustín too. You all have family nearby. I don't. I feel empty inside. I don't think I can stay here much longer. Or, being completely honest, maybe I can, but not with Agustín."

Eden wanted to add, not with Eva and Edwardo either, deciding doing that would have been too honest.

"I am jealous because you, Edwardo, and Agustín have family you enjoy being with, because you want to spend time with them, not because you have to. Your lives are complete, mine is not."

More than a little surprised at what Eden just told her, Eva struggled to respond.

"Eden, I know you're not from here, but you can visit your family with or without Agustín, right? Or they could come here to see you."

"No, Eva, I have no family; that's the problem. Why I don't is not important. I've not found a way to fill that void here in Gràcia, or maybe anywhere in Spain. And while it's not his fault, I probably can't do that with Agustín. The boys look like they're about to come back. Remember, do not tell anyone what I just told you; you promised."

Eva nodded, forcing herself to look happy despite feeling the opposite. Edwardo and Agustín sat down, laughing loudly, apparently unaware of the change in both Eva and Eden from when they left to go to the bar. Agustín spoke.

"Bueno, ¿Quién está listo para un poco más de vino? and for my beautiful Eden, more wine, sweets?"

Eva could see that Eden was very uncomfortable, especially because Agustín was drunk, and Edwardo was no better. She decided to take matters into her own hands.

"Don't open that wine, boys, save it for another time. We've had enough; you both have, too. It's time to go home."

Edwardo and Agustín were surprised by this sudden turn of events. When they left the table to get more wine at the bar, everything seemed fine. Now that was no longer the case, and something about how Eva said what she did, along with the serious look on Eden's face, told them it was best to do as they were told.

CHAPTER THIRTY

Eden looked around, hoping to see something she recognized, something to help her understand her situation. As before, the room was empty except for four overstuffed leather chairs, each with a small table beside it, cups of coffee on each table with steam rising from them. Three chairs arranged in a narrow half-circle facing the one chair in which Eden now sat, immediately joined by Giáp, Raymond, and Shelly in the other three, all now back in Other Worlds.

"Will I feel better once this is over?"

"What will make you feel better, Eden?" Giáp asked.

Eden didn't answer, thinking to herself, *If I knew what would make me feel better, I wouldn't be here.*

"Eden, Shelly and I know you are struggling. We understand the discussion you had with Eva. That's why we are here with you now."

Eden looked up, her expression rigid, angry.

"That's why you're here with me now? To tell me again how we're all 'connected,' how I am not alone? But I am alone, aren't I? I believe I am in Gràcia with Agustín, my friends, all of whom have family—real family, not just ghosts of people who are no longer alive."

She looked to her left as if she had heard something in that direction. Seeing nothing, she stood up and turned away from Giáp, Shelly, and Raymond. Where there had been nothing before, she now saw a white spiral void that seemed to go on forever. She recognized Giáp's voice.

"What does that mean to you, Eden? The white void: what is that to you?"

Eden was transfixed, unable to take her eyes off it, now spiraling inward as if it would pull her into the vortex, spinning faster and faster. Her mind commanded her to run, but she couldn't move. The white vortex, a deep guttural hum, a point of light at its center growing brighter. One split second, she felt she could find it, the next...

Eden floated through a white darkness, glimpsing faint figures she thought she recognized, approaching her, then quickly moving away. Fragments of lives she might have lived or could still live if she made the right choices swiftly appeared and vanished. A young child drawing pictures on her parents' driveway with colored chalk. In another, a young woman acting as if the life she lives is the one she envisioned for herself. And finally, an old woman with less time ahead than behind, now trying to live that which never was. A pulsating world she both loved and hated.

Am I dead?

No, Eden, you are searching for what you never had, what you never will have.

My life?

Your life as you wished it to be. A life that never happened. You won't find what never existed. Accept that is so, and you can return to your search for what can exist.

As suddenly as she was pulled into the white vortex, she felt herself slam into the chair she had been sitting in, back in Other Worlds. The room echoed as if struck by thunder, with sound and sight reverberations forcing Eden to close her eyes and tightly cover her ears to block out the noise until...silence.

Her eyes still closed, she waited, hoping the oppressive noise would stop. Hearing nothing, she slowly opened her eyes. The room was empty, except for the three overstuffed leather chairs facing her, which once again were occupied by Giáp, Shelly, and Raymond.

I turned you back, Eden.

"Turned me back? From where? Where was I?

Giáp answered with his voice rather than with his thoughts.

"You were in the void you desperately want to fill. But you can't, and no one can do it for you. That is the mortal life you never lived. You can go back to it if you wish, as you believe it would have been. If you do, you will be there forever—no second chances. Raymond and Shelly can tell you about the void; they've been through it too. Every soul does both before being born into mortal life and again after leaving it, before finding their eternal existence. The only ones who don't are those who, like you, were meant to live a mortal life but never did. Like you, they must find their immortal existence. Not all try, possibly including you. Those who don't must exist forever in the spiral white void you experienced.

Eternity experiencing what I just went through? Unfathomable!

But you know now it isn't, don't you, Eden? You don't understand what your eternal life might be because you keep looking for what your mortal life would have been if you had been born. You must choose one or the other. Failing to choose is still a choice. Think carefully.

Broken emotionally and spiritually, Eden started to cry uncontrollably, gasping as she struggled to put her thoughts into words.

How can I feel so much pain when I have never been born?

You do because you have slipped from almost living into a place most souls briefly inhabit after mortal death. A place where they determine what their immortality will be. They don't need to choose; they are where they wish to be. You want to deny that you are. You feel pain because you have, in some ways, lived a mortal existence.

But why do I have to face this alone?

You are not alone, Eden. Shelly and I are with you. As Giáp said, we have been in the white void, just as you are now. We found each other there, believing we had discovered our eternal existence. We learned it could be, but only if we left you to your void. We rejected what we thought we wanted to become. We chose to connect with you as your parents. And now, as we must do, you need to decide. Reject our offer to help and resume your search on your own. If you do, we wish you well. Or join us in searching for our immortality, now including yours—a family in the multiverse. The choice is yours, Eden.

CHAPTER THIRTY-ONE

"ARE YOU SURE, EDEN?"

"I am, Agustín, and I know you are too. We've known this was coming for a while, but I want you to know I care about you deeply and always will. I'm not sure we were ever in love, whatever that is. I doubt we ever would be. We are not those people. Can I ask what your plans are?"

"I will keep practicing photography. I'm not making enough money just from that; I also need to work at something else. I've signed a two-year contract to teach Spanish to wealthy tourists in São Sebastião, Brazil. Not far down the coast from Rio de Janeiro, near São Paulo. A spot popular with Americans and Canadians who like to boast to friends back home about their experiences in what they call the 'real Brazil.' From what I know, it's a very comfortable seaside resort town. Tourists think that learning Spanish will be more useful when they go home than learning Portuguese would be. My job is to give them lessons while they're on vacation. Not the bohemian, artistic life we talked about so much. What about you?"

"Good question, I wish I knew. I will keep developing my pencil art, hoping to shift from tourist sales to a more established career. Hmm. Imagine me saying that, as if I were still a young woman in my early twenties arriving in Gràcia. Not anymore, not for quite some time now. So I need to either grow my art career or do what you're doing and find a different path."

Agustín poured them each a glass of wine, lifting his in a toast to them both.

"Brindo por ti, mi amor. Que el buen tiempo, el buen vino y Dios te acompañen dondequiera que vayas."

"The same and more to you, mi amor."

CHAPTER THIRTY-TWO

Agustín's departure a month earlier left scars Eden had not anticipated. She missed him, accepting that they would never be together again. She kept up her routine, displaying her pencil art on the street and earning a modest reputation as an artist who might someday achieve greater success. She still had her friends, including Eva, who had separated from Edwardo. They comforted each other, attempting to convince themselves that both breakups were for the best, each secretly harboring doubts that was true.

A typical warm summer day in Gràcia, one Eden wished she could spend doing something other than working. She set up her easel and displayed her pencil drawings for sale on Travessera de Gràcia. Foot traffic was light that day, and instead of watching for potential customers, she started sketching a nondescript building on the other side of the avenue.

"Your work is beautiful. You have amazing talent!"

Eden looked up and saw an Asian man she judged to be about her age, peering over her shoulder at her drawing, less than halfway finished. She hadn't heard him approach; he seemed to appear out of nowhere.

"Thank you. I hope everyone who sees my art feels the way you say you do. However, judging by how many buy some of it, I assume that isn't the case."

"Unfortunately, I can't afford to buy either, but I appreciate your talent. My name is An."

"Good to meet you, An, I'm Eden."

"You have no accent. Are you Spanish?"

"No," Eden sighed, "I'm a little bit from everywhere too much so to be from anywhere. What about you?"

An laughed, "I like that. Can I not be from anywhere as well?"

"Of course, why not?"

Eden found An interesting. She wanted to ask where in Asia he was from, but decided not to, thinking it might be intrusive.

"You see what I do for a living, An. What do you do?"

"What I do, or what I make money from to live? They are not the same."

"You answer my questions with questions. Are you a mystic?"

An smiled before answering.

"Yes, we are all different in wonderful ways. Are you here every day? I want to keep talking with you. And maybe soon I will have enough money to truly honor your talent by buying something from you."

"I am somewhere along here most days except Wednesdays. You don't have to buy anything. I appreciate the break from drawing. Enjoy the rest of your day, An. I hope to see you soon."

"You too, Eden, and you will see me again soon."

CHAPTER THIRTY-THREE

Eden saw An much sooner than she expected. It wouldn't have surprised her if she never saw him again, but here he was, like the day before, appearing seemingly out of nowhere. She was still working on the drawing of the building across the street, this time from a slightly different vantage point.

"That is a better perspective. It highlights the building's strength," he said.

"An!" Eden said, surprised by his unexpected appearance. "Once again, I did not see you coming. How do you do that?"

An just smiled, looking at her drawing, as Eden looked at the building, comparing the two.

"The building's strength. I realize buildings need to be strong, but I never thought of it the way you do when thinking about a person's strength." She looked again at her drawing before continuing. "I think you're right, it is a strong building, it does have strength."

"Most would think, as you did, that strength is only for living things. That building lives. I don't mean in the traditional sense, but in its own way. Your easel does too— if it didn't, you couldn't create your art."

Eden stopped working on her drawing and looked up at An. She found him to be so different from others she had met in Spain or anywhere else, for that matter.

There is something both strange and beautiful about him. He perceives things differently than most, just as I would like to do when drawing inanimate objects like this building.

"I see what you mean, but I wouldn't have on my own. I will try to do that more often when choosing what to draw. Thank you."

"My pleasure, Eden. Are you hungry? It's almost lunchtime. How about soup at a cozy café just a block or so from here?"

"Sounds good, and when we're finished, I need to come back to complete this drawing from this spot. I look forward to doing so now with a fresh perspective on the building's strength," she said, starting to pack up her drawing supplies.

"Of course. We won't be long. When you start again, have you considered the building's gender? If you had, you wouldn't refer to it as 'it.' You would say 'her' or 'him'."

Hearing this, Shelly laughed.

"No, I did not. It was enough for me to have even thought of it possessing strength," she said, turning to study the building again. "But now that you mention it, the building is female."

"Very good, Eden. Your appreciation for inanimate objects has expanded greatly in the short time we've been talking. You will see this manifested in your art."

"Thank you, An, but you didn't say whether it was female or male. Which is it for you?"

"As with beauty, all descriptors we apply to objects are in the eye of the beholder."

Lunch was just as An said it would be: nearby and reasonably priced. Eden enjoyed the sopa de ajo and sobado bread—especially with a glass of red wine. It was a nice break from drawing. Still, what Eden really appreciated was having lunch with An. She wanted to get to know him better.

"An, you didn't answer when I asked yesterday where you are from. It's okay if you'd rather not say, but I am curious."

"Oh, but I did, Eden, as you did. Like you, I, too, am from anywhere," he said, smiling, tearing off a piece of sobado, dipping it in his soup.

"I did forget that, didn't I?"

"But I believe you prefer I be a little more specific, yes? I was born in Vietnam during Chiến tranh Việt Nam, Vietnamese for Resistance War against America. I've been away from Vietnam for over a year now, traveling, experiencing the world. Like you, I am young, but I already know there is far too much for me to see in one short lifetime. I am doing my best to see as much of it as I can. You also being from anywhere," he smiled at Eden, "can you be more specific where that might be for you?"

Eden immediately regretted asking where An was from, knowing he would almost certainly ask her the same thing — a question she could only answer honestly.

"I would tell you if I knew. The fact is, I don't, and I have no family to ask. I assume I was adopted, but by whom I don't know. Like you, I am now a young adult. You would think I would know something of my background. I don't."

The smile now gone from his face, An replied.

"It seems we share that in common, too, Eden, or something very similar. My father was forced to serve as a soldier in the Northern army. My mother told me she never heard from or about him again after he left to fight the South Vietnamese and American armies. She assumes he was killed in combat, but she doesn't know how or what happened to his body. I prefer to think of him as existing in this universe or in some other one. I can't see him, but I know he's not dead."

"I'm really sorry, An. I've spent too much time feeling sorry for myself. Your story reminds me that many others have similar experiences, and some are even worse. You're right; we do have a lot in common. Do you at least know your father's name?"

"I do; Đoàn ăn Giáp."

Their lunch ended, An and Eden promised to meet again soon. Eden was happy; she found something special about him and looked forward to getting to know him better.

CHAPTER THIRTY-FOUR

I need your help, Eden.

What do you want me to do?

Tell An I am fine. Tell him he is right; I am not dead. My soul exists in a universe parallel to the one he lives in.

Can't you tell him that?

Not at this time. Please do that for me. Will you?

Eden had no memory of leaving Other Worlds the last time she was there with Raymond, Shelly, and Giáp. Now, back again, alone, this time only with Giáp, sitting in the two leather chairs facing each other.

I will do what I can to help, but you must tell me more. An will want to know how I came to know this. How do I answer him?

You need to reassure him without making him wonder how you know about me. Over time, you'll be able to speak openly. I will too, but not right now. The two of you did not find each other by chance. You were meant to be together to show him that I exist. He told you he prefers to believe I do, but he isn't entirely convinced. He's lost, having never had a father to guide him through life. Reassure him that I am okay and that he will be too.

I want to help, but I don't know what to do. How can I reassure An about something so personal he doesn't know, while I do?

He will, Eden, because the two of you are much more connected than you realize. You are a nexus among Raymond, Shelly, me, and now An. You will know what to say and when, so he hears what he needs to hear. Will you help me help my son?

Eden woke up, wanting to sleep longer.

Why am I so tired? I didn't feel this exhausted when I went to bed. Now I feel as if I have been awake all night. What did I dream? Giáp! I dreamed I was back in Other Worlds with Giáp. He wants me to assure An that he is fine and that he is right to believe the father he never knew is doing well. My God, how do I do that?

You will know what to say, when to say it, and how to say it. Will you help me help my son?

That was no dream.

An and Eden arranged their schedules to be near each other throughout the day. Eden did pencil drawings while An took photos of the same scene. They often sold both to tourists who found the combination compelling. They were both making more money than they had on their own, enjoying themselves more together. An told Eden about growing up in Vietnam, raised by his mother. He had been away almost a year now. He would go back to visit her at some point, but not now, particularly since meeting and growing close to Eden.

Their conversations prompted Eden to explore Vietnamese culture and art. She became captivated by many aspects, notably silk and eggshell paintings. She would mimic what she saw in pencil drawings. An enjoyed what he was doing and tried to create his own eggshell paintings. Initially, he and Eden felt these might not have commercial value, but as he practiced, his work improved. He had another idea.

"Eden, we are doing fairly well here in Gràcia."

"Fairly well? I should say so. I'm selling twice as much as I did when I randomly picked a scene to draw in pencil. People are willing to pay more for that and for my pencil interpretation of your photography. We are doing very well!"

An wasn't sure whether what he wanted to say next would be met with enthusiasm. He feared Eden might prefer to keep working in Barcelona. But having come this far, he would go the rest of the way.

"I never expected to stay in Barcelona as long as I have, now almost three years. Did you?"

"Now that you ask, no, I didn't. Are you going somewhere else?"

"Nowhere without you. I have a suggestion. We have a growing reputation for our combined work. We receive inquiries from all over the world from people who own what we created, asking if we can do something specific for them. We could do this anywhere in the world. Why don't we move somewhere else? A place we would want to live for an extended period, creating new pencil and photography art about that place? We have a large customer mailing list. Many would buy more when they learn of our new creations."

Eden put her pencil down and pushed her chair back from the easel. Her expression told An that she couldn't believe what he had just proposed.

"Think about it before you reject the idea; there's a lot we would need to figure out. How would we handle the art and customer contacts? How much more would we need to sell to justify the expense of moving to a new location? Things like that."

Eden smiled at An before responding.

"I wasn't thinking about any of that. My first thought was, where do we want to move to? My second thought was, for how long, before moving on to wherever is next. I have a suggestion for how to handle customer contacts if you care to hear it."

Surprised, An nodded.

"Your mother is relatively young, in good health, and always asks about our work. She is active, articulate, and fluent in Vietnamese, English, and French. Why don't you tell her what we plan to do?" An noticed Eden left no doubt about his suggestion. "Ask whether she would be willing to handle the back-office side of our business so we can focus on creating the art. If our sales continue to grow as they have, her income will increase as well. Good for us, good for her."

"Eden, I was prepared to hear you say you wanted no part of my suggestion. I never expected you to take what I said as far as you have, given how little you knew. I have to ask: are you certain you agree to do this? I don't want you to go along with me because you feel you have no choice. It is a big step for both of us, and for my mother, if she were to be involved."

"It is a risk, and we have much more to work out before you take this to your mother. However, I have a question for you. Assume for the moment I had rejected your proposal and said I would stay here. Where would you go?"

"I already told you. Nowhere without you."

CHAPTER THIRTY-FIVE

ALONG WITH WORKING HARD AND EXPANDING THEIR BUSINESS, EDEN AND An devised a plan to do even more. They would publicly announce their artist residency in three locations for six months each, starting on the first day of the new year. They called Linh, An's mother, to explain their plans and asked whether she would agree to handle all customer contacts, including marketing, sales, and shipping, for the works created by Eden and An. Linh was very excited to be part of it, especially when An told her that Eden suggested they spend two weeks with her at her home in Hội An, preparing for their joint business venture.

The day arrived for Eden and An to fly to Tan Son Nhat Airport near Ho Chi Minh City, formerly known as Saigon. After clearing customs, they headed to Ga Sài Gòn train station to catch the Reunification Express for the overnight trip to Da Nang.

"We're close now, Eden. This time tomorrow night, we will be at my mother's house. I'm happy, and she is too, especially because you suggested we do this. She knows something about you from our phone conversations. But meeting you and hearing that you said we should take time to be together as a family means a lot to her. Thank you again, Eden."

"I'm looking forward to meeting your mother and spending time with her. I'm sure she can teach me a lot about Vietnamese culture. But I'm a little sad, too. I wish I had family you could meet."

An saw Eden's mood had darkened. He hoped to change the subject to make her feel better.

"Have you ever slept on a train? This one might be a bit rough."

"I haven't. This is my first, but I'm so tired after almost twenty-four hours awake getting this far. I don't think I'll have any trouble sleeping."

Both had planned to stay awake for at least the first hour or so once underway. Eden was asleep before the train left the station, as was An soon after.

CHAPTER THIRTY-SIX

Around the same time it took to fly from Barcelona to Ho Chi Minh City, the Reunification Express train arrived at Da Nang station. Linh was there to greet An and Eden. She quickly hugged An, then turned to face Eden, who stood to the side. Bowing slightly, she spoke.

"I am so honored that you wanted to come to Vietnam to meet me, Eden, and to bring my son home to me, even if only for a short while."

"Con rất vinh dự được gặp mẹ và rất vui khi được gặp An. Xin hãy tha thứ cho nỗ lực kém cỏi của tôi khi nói tiếng Việt."

Linh and An were shocked to hear Eden speak Vietnamese.

"I had no idea. How long have you been studying Vietnamese, Eden?" An said, equally as surprised as was Linh.

"It wasn't very good, but I wanted to try anyway."

"You have nothing to apologize for, Eden. You did much more than try. I am so honored," Linh said, wiping away tears. "My car is close by. Let me carry your suitcase for you, Eden," she said, reaching for the nearest one.

"Thank you, Linh. It's not heavy, and I'm well rested from the train trip last night. I'll carry it."

An carried the other two, and the three of them started for Linh's car. Once there, the luggage loaded, they began the little more than half-hour ride to Linh's home in Hội An.

"I've only been away a short while, but so much has changed," An said, looking out the window from the back seat. "I hope Hội An is as I remember it."

"It is, son. There have been some changes, some of which I don't like, but it will mostly be as you remember."

Sitting in the front seat next to Linh, Eden commented. "I've been reading and studying about Vietnam since the war. I know there have been many changes due to economic growth. I am most interested in Vietnamese art, and am very happy to learn that Hội An is an art center, a beautiful place to live and work. You are very fortunate to live here, Linh."

"I agree. There are trade-offs to consider. We don't have the large shopping districts of Da Nang and Hue, nor anything like those of Hanoi and Saigon. But that's why we've preserved the city's ancient charm and the surrounding area. Driving to Da Nang or Hue for an occasional shopping trip isn't a problem."

"Thank you for complimenting my poor Vietnamese, Linh. An told me you are fluent in English. I can see that you are. Where did you learn to speak it so well?"

"My father owned a business in Saigon. He was able to afford private Western education for my two brothers and me. It was there that I learned to speak English, practicing it at home while speaking Vietnamese with my friends."

"Two brothers. Do they live near you?"

"One lives in Hue, not far away. I see him and his family fairly often. He knows the two of you are here and looks forward to seeing you, An, and meeting you, Eden. Unfortunately, my older brother was killed by the Vietcong during the battle for Hue. I should say, murdered by them; he was not a soldier. The Vietcong murdered many young men they believed might fight for the South, either immediately or at some point in the future."

"Linh, I am so sorry to hear that. I didn't know; I wouldn't have asked if I had known."

"I understand, Eden, but please do not feel sorry for me. Vietnamese women of my generation have lost much during and after the war. Children, fathers, mothers, wives," she paused, "...husbands. An's father also died in the war, conscripted to fight for the communists against the South and the Americans. His loyalty was to the South, but had he refused, they would have killed him, me, and all our family. He did as they ordered, and he was killed in the fighting. I say he was killed. I don't know for certain. He never returned. If he is dead, I do not know what happened to his body. I was pregnant with An. I forced myself to focus on raising him. I had to put my grief away for another time."

Linh continued driving, saying nothing more. Eden looked at An in the back seat, his head down, as if deliberately avoiding eye contact with her. He had only told her that his father had been an NVA soldier killed in the war. Nothing about the rest of her family, its politics, or that one of her uncles had been murdered by the Vietcong.

An has told me very little about his life and his family. What else will I learn?

CHAPTER THIRTY-SEVEN

TWO DAYS AFTER ARRIVING IN HỘI AN, EDEN AND AN SETTLED INTO Linh's comfortable home in the Cẩm Thanh district of the city. Walking distance to restaurants, shopping, and services, including those Linh would need to arrange for shipping the art Eden and An would create and sell to customers around the world.

An spent time with his mother, but only a fraction of the time Eden and Linh were together. Linh did what most future mothers-in-law do: she told her prospective daughter-in-law what it was like to raise An as a single, widowed mother. This bothered Eden more than it seemed to bother Linh.

She said she and the women of her generation have endured much grief. It hasn't hardened her; she has compartmentalized it and made sense of what makes no sense.

During one of their daily conversations, Linh decided she had shared enough about herself, possibly too much. It was time for Eden to answer questions about her family. Eden expected this and was ready to respond.

"No, I don't mind you asking, Linh, and thank you for sharing so much about your family with me. I have nothing so dramatic to say regarding mine. You don't know everything about your family — including what happened to your husband. I know nothing about my family. I assume I was orphaned, but I have no basis for that. However, for no apparent reason, I've increasingly felt as though I either do know some of it or soon will. An has never questioned me in detail about my family. It came up only once. I told him something similar to what I'm telling you. He didn't ask again. No one has. I've now admitted to you what I haven't to An. I feel I will soon know more. I hope so; not knowing is frustrating."

Eden looked up at Linh and smiled.

"One reason I suggested we come visit you is that I envied An for having you so emotionally close while being physically apart. I looked forward to meeting you, Linh, being close to you, and becoming part of your family. I hope you don't mind."

Linh reached for a handkerchief to wipe a tear from her eye.

"Eden, only close Vietnamese family members hug each other; we don't do that with people we aren't extremely close to. May I hug you?" she said, standing in front of Eden.

Eden stood up to face her. "Of course you may, Linh."

They held their embrace for over a minute, each recognizing this moment as a turning point in their relationship. Two women from vastly different backgrounds and cultures, sharing something in very different ways. From now on, things would be different.

"Linh, I have a favor to ask."

"Certainly, Eden, whatever you like."

"If it is all right with you, would you mind me calling you Mother?"

CHAPTER THIRTY-EIGHT

THE TWO WEEKS EDEN AND AN STAYED WITH HIS MOTHER PASSED QUICKLY. The three of them wished they had time to show Eden some of Vietnam, starting with Hội An. But the need to set Linh up to handle the backroom duties for Eden and An's growing art business made it impossible. They assured Linh they would return at least once a year, next year, putting vacation time at the top of their list.

"I'm almost packed. How are you doing, An?"

"Almost finished. I'll be ready to catch the train back to Saigon this evening. I know my mother is sad to see us leave, but she seems excited about managing our business affairs. Good for us, good for her. We don't have to worry about it, and she makes a good living doing it."

"You're right. Not knowing your mother, I had some concerns when we arrived. What if she didn't seem able or willing to do it? We'd have to start over and find a way to complete the business side. But she is a very accomplished woman; I can't imagine a better choice than Linh."

Eden put down the last of the clothes she was folding to pack into her suitcase, glancing around the room where An grew up, now updated for adults.

"An, you slept in this room as a child. When you look around now, it is decorated very differently. What goes through your mind?"

An stopped packing, and looked at Eden, smiling.

“Funny, you would ask that. I was here alone the other morning. Mother was cooking Bò Né for breakfast, and the smells drifted down the hall into my room. I wasn't thinking about growing up in this room until I caught the scent of the beef and eggs. I stood at the open door behind you, listening for the sizzle of the meat in the hot cast-iron pan, just as I had when I was a little boy. I looked around the room, now so different, and imagined everything as it had been so long ago. I remembered so much of my life here, my actions, my thoughts, and worries. The room is completely different now, but that aroma took me back to a moment in time that's gone.”

“But not gone forever, An. You love that aroma so much it transports you back to your youth. I envy you. I recall nothing of my childhood—no house I grew up in, no cooking scents.” She paused—“Nothing about family, my mother or father. It's as if I have amnesia about my past. Maybe that's exactly what it is, amnesia. I've never thought of that before, but that would explain why my past is a void.”

An closed his suitcase and sat down on the bed next to Eden.

"Is that why you told me you were from 'anywhere' when we first met?"

"I don't know if I want to talk about this.” She paused before continuing. “Yes, it is. I'm embarrassed; people will either think there's something wrong with me if I can't recall even basic things, or maybe I do, and I'm hiding something from them. Be honest, didn't one or the other occur to you when we talked about our pasts?"

"No, I just assumed you would tell me whatever you wanted me to know and keep private what you didn't."

"Your mother answered all my many questions, some of which I probably shouldn't have asked. She is a very strong woman, and I have great respect for her. I assumed she would ask similar questions about my family, and when she did, I was prepared to answer truthfully. I had become so comfortable with her that it didn't bother me as it had when others asked."

"You told her you remember very little of your early life? Did you refer to it as amnesia?"

"I did tell her I do not recall any of it. I did not call it amnesia; that hadn't occurred to me until now."

Having now said it twice, sitting in this room, An's childhood room, hearing his memories, Eden could not put aside her questioning whether she had some form of amnesia. If so, what, if anything, could she do about it? Was she willing to look for answers, a quest that would necessarily interfere with their art residency business as soon as they left Hội An?

"We'd better finish packing and get ready to go. The train won't wait for us."

CHAPTER THIRTY-NINE

As before, Eden felt herself floating through the same white, spiraling void she had found so disconcerting the first time. The difference now was that she knew she was on her way back to Other Worlds.

Who will be waiting for me this time? I'm actually looking forward to being there; I have more questions I would like answered.

In less time than it took Eden to think that thought, without searching for it, she reached for the cup of coffee she knew would be on the table next to the overstuffed leather chair she sat in. As she picked up the cup, watching steam rise, she told herself to savor every moment of this latest visit to Other Worlds.

I want to remember everything. If I have amnesia about my past, so be it. But I will *remember all that happens to me now and in the future. I was in Vietnam with An and his mother, Linh. We were there to visit and prepare Linh to handle our business affairs. We did that, and Linh and I spoke candidly about our pasts. An and I finally did as well, though not as much as I did with his mother. I remember all that. Can I only recall what others remember about me? Am I living through their memories? Do I have any of my own?*

The more Eden tried to understand her situation, the more agitated she became.

What in God's name do *I know for certain?*

"You came here on your own, Eden. I did not summon you, nor did

Shelly or Raymond. You came because you have questions you believe we can answer."

The same pulsating sounds she had heard before filled her mind with images she recognized from her first visit to Other Worlds. Glimpses of a childhood she never experienced, brief glimpses of Raymond and Shelly, the parents she never knew. She sat comfortably, unafraid of what or whom she would find waiting for her. She saw Giáp, Raymond, and Shelly, initially faint, growing clearer the more she opened her eyes.

Questions I want answered. Yes, there are.

Eden opened her eyes wide, immediately noticing Giáp, Raymond, and Shelly seated in chairs just like the one she was in, their faces staring back at her, expressionless and unmoving. For the first time, Eden wondered whether they were even real, unsure what "real" meant in Other Worlds.

"Ask whatever you wish, Eden. We will answer," a voice said, one that did not obviously come from any of the four of them in the room.

"I saw faint, partial images of myself as a child before settling into this chair," she said, deliberately slapping the padded armrest to emphasize her point. "I saw colorful chalk drawings I made on the driveway of my parents' home—your home, Raymond, Shelly. If I were never born, how could I see that? Why do I see your images fading in and out, floating, images of me as a child? You say I was never born, yet I see myself. You were born, Raymond; if you hadn't been, you couldn't have been killed in a war you never fought. You, Shelly, could never have gone to Singapore to meet him or taken your own life if you hadn't been born."

"Eden, those images you see of yourself, of me, and Raymond are the three of us searching for our places in the multiverse. We are lost. You are lost. You called out to me because I would have been your mother. I heard you. That happened despite my no longer living, you never being mortally born. Neither Raymond nor I was aware of you in your search. You would have been our child had we not died. Giáp said we must choose to either ignore your call for help and continue to exist in what we thought was our immortal, eternal existence, or abandon our immortality to help you in your search. We are here to help you, Eden."

Eden paused to consider what Shelly had said. Nothing new; she had heard this before from Giáp. But now, hearing it again while experiencing the white spiral void, this time in a less threatening way, made it all feel more real.

"If we have not found our immortal lives, what must we do?"

"Your search will answer that question for you, Eden, and for you as well, Shelly and Raymond."

CHAPTER FORTY

Before visiting An's mother in Vietnam, Eden and An had planned to start their artist residency in one of several major European cities. However, after further consideration, they switched plans and chose Singapore as their first stop. They did so because Singapore is a popular tourist destination, especially for wealthy visitors from the East and West, many of whom they believed would appreciate their unique pencil art and photography. Additionally, it was only a two-hour flight to Ho Chi Minh City. It was better to stay near Linh in case she faced issues and needed help from one or both of them during her first year in her new role.

Eden and An were fortunate to find an available and affordable apartment within walking distance of Tivoli Gardens, a major tourist destination for dining and shopping. Once settled in, they quickly returned to their previous routine, creating, presenting, and selling their art, with a few differences from what they had expected, one in particular.

Having become more established than just being street vendors, they thought it would be a good idea to open a gallery near where tourists congregate. However, having researched rental properties that would suit them, they found the idea prohibitively expensive and likely of little value. They saw very few tourists visiting local galleries.

Instead, Eden and An returned to their old ways, showing their art in parks, on sidewalks, and side streets where tourists could not miss their creations. Along with creating new pencil drawings and photos of nearby famous Singapore locations, their sales increased significantly over those in Gràcia. Enough so that they promised themselves they would take two days off midweek, working the other five days to be available when potential customers were most likely to be interested in seeing their art.

After a day visiting Pulau Ubin Island across from Changi Beach Park, they decided to do as tourists would and visit Lau Pa Sat for dinner outside, enjoying a reasonably comfortable, low-humidity evening.

"Did you have fun today? I certainly did. Well, everything except the mosquitoes; they were terrible."

Eden laughed as she examined the bites on her forearm.

"Yes, there were." Her expression suddenly grew more serious as she looked directly at An. "I don't know if it's just me, but I find something strange about many places we've been in and around Singapore, including Palau Ubin and a little area around here as well," she said, glancing at tables filled with diners, all seeming to enjoy dinner outside on a night with comfortable heat and humidity. "Do you feel any of that?"

"Strange?" he said, using his knife and fork to explore the plate of food the waiter had set in front of him. "Right now, the only thing I find strange is wondering what this is. I ordered fish, didn't I? Does this look like fish to you? " he said, continuing to probe his dinner.

"Stop playing with your food, An. You are Vietnamese; you would eat anything that walked, crawled, flew, or swam near you. I'm not talking about food. I had a strange feeling on the island today, and I feel it again here. Don't laugh. It's as if ghosts are nearby, watching us."

This last comment caused An to set down his utensils before answering Eden.

"Okay, ghosts. I haven't, and I don't now. But if I did, the ghosts would probably be the result of the Japanese occupation of Singapore during the war—a terrible time, especially for ethnic Chinese. I'm not Chinese. I didn't grow up here, but I did in Vietnam, which was also brutally oppressed by the Japanese. Many Vietnamese people who were alive then and were still around as I was growing up spoke of ghosts—both Japanese and Vietnamese, still fighting for control of each other's souls. I didn't believe it there, and I don't here, but that's all I can offer about the strangeness you say you feel. Can we eat now?"

Eden agreed, though she was still thinking about how she felt since coming to Singapore. It wasn't Japanese; something or someone was watching her.

CHAPTER FORTY-ONE

Why do I feel I'm being watched? Is something evil stalking me?

Nothing evil, Eden. Raymond and I are watching you. Giáp is too. You chose Singapore for your business for a reason, but not the one you think. You will achieve great success there, but it is about more than business. You have unknowingly followed Raymond's and my footsteps. We have been to many of the places you have been. Raymond, only while exploring his unlived life; me, in both the life I lived unhappily—sad because he wasn't with me—and another with him, both of us searching for our immortality. Do not fear this feeling. You can learn from it if you embrace your emotions.

You say Giáp is watching me as well. Why would he? He has no direct connection to me.

That is true, Eden. I do not have a direct connection with you, but I do with An. He will soon feel as you do. If he questions it, I will help him understand its meaning. Ultimately, you both must understand, each in your own time and way.

CHAPTER FORTY-TWO

"How did you sleep?" An asked as Eden entered the kitchen, finding him drinking coffee. "Can I pour you a cup?"

"Yes, please. Sleep? Not very well at all. Do you remember me asking at dinner whether you found anything about Singapore to be strange?" she asked as she sat at the table, accepting the cup of coffee An held out to her.

"Yes, certainly. Is that what your dream was about?"

"I suppose, in a way, and yet... Have you ever dreamed something so vividly that you believed it had to be true when you woke up? That happened to me. I almost woke you to tell you about it."

"I'd like to say that would have been okay, but I'm glad you didn't. I was exhausted and slept well. I'm not so sure that would have happened if I had listened to more of your ghost stories in the middle of the night. What was it about?"

Eden was pleased that An wanted to hear about her dream. She desperately wanted to tell someone.

"I dreamed I was in an extraordinary room, with walls that spiraled like fluid, not solid, and no furniture except the leather chair I was sitting in and a small table beside it. A deep, low-frequency hum pulsed, filling the space. I was in a strange coffee shop; I even dreamed of the name—Other Worlds Coffee. I felt something bad was watching me. Three people responded in my thoughts, telling me who they were and that they were watching out for me to help me."

"That doesn't sound so bad, certainly better than being watched by ghosts."

Eden looked at An, a dead-serious expression on her face. "Call them what you like, all three were dead."

Now it was An's facial expression that was serious.

"Go on, what did they say?"

"You might laugh, but don't! I'm in no mood for ridicule. If you find this funny, keep it to yourself, end of conversation. Two of them would have been my parents. I thought something was strange about the places we'd been, something evil. These two, whoever or whatever they were, said they had been watching me to help me in my search. I didn't know what they meant by my 'search.' They said I must embrace my feelings, not fear them, if I am to learn more."

"I'm not laughing, Eden. What did they say about me?"

"They didn't, but a third person, an entity of some sort—I don't know what to call it—spoke to me about you. He said he has a direct connection to you, just as the other two have with me. The three of them are somehow connected, which means the five of us are in a way I do not understand."

An did not know what to think, but Eden did. She had no doubt it represented something real, something tied to her feeling that the places they visited in Singapore held personal significance for her. She questioned whether to tell An about her previous dreams. She had dismissed some of them as inconsequential, but now thought they might be very real.

Dreaming about Giáp, by name, before meeting An, isn't a coincidence. But what does it mean?

It is time for all of us to meet, Eden.

CHAPTER FORTY-THREE

EDEN COULDN'T STOP THINKING ABOUT OTHER WORLDS, SHELLY, Raymond, and, most importantly, Giáp. She struggled to imagine what he would think. This, along with the growing certainty that it was all somehow connected to her strange feelings about Singapore, weighed heavily on her. She knew what she had to do.

As they usually did on Wednesdays, An and Eden spent time away from central Singapore, where they worked. Eden appreciated Singapore's beauty, and although it was accessible to much larger Malaysia and other Southeast Asian countries, she increasingly felt the world around her was falling apart.

With breakfast now over, they decided to spend the day at the Chinese Garden, known for its plant and concrete animal sculptures, waterways, and graceful bridges, offering many places to escape Singapore's busy pace and enjoy peaceful serenity. Something Eden desperately needed.

They paused briefly atop the thirteen-arch White Rainbow Bridge, looking down at the water below. So peaceful. Eden decided this was the right moment and place to tell An everything she had been hiding from him.

"I appreciate that you didn't laugh at me the other day when I shared my dream."

"I saw you were serious and troubled, Eden. I would never have laughed at you."

"Thank you. I appreciate that. But there is more I need you to know, much of it involving you. I ask that you listen to everything I have to say before asking questions or making comments. I need to get it all out before you respond. Agreed?"

An knew he had no choice; he nodded and answered, "Agreed!"

"My dream the other night wasn't the first; there have been others very similar since we moved to Singapore. That's coupled with a feeling I have when we visit certain places." She paused, looking around. "Something I can't explain. I don't know if I should even continue telling you this; you may think I've lost my mind."

"I don't think so, Eden. I could see you were troubled soon after we arrived. You need to tell me what's wrong. I want to know so I can help you."

An's words encouraged Eden, and she continued.

"As I told you the other day, I visit Other Worlds Coffee in my dreams, where I meet Shelly and Raymond. A third person tells me they would have been my parents." She paused again, wondering what An would think of her after hearing the rest. She knew she had to keep going.

"They would have been my parents if Raymond, a US soldier, hadn't been killed forty-six years earlier in the Vietnam War. Shelly and Raymond had been exchanging letters. He suddenly stopped writing, and she had no way of knowing what had happened to him. She was so upset she committed suicide five years later. If that were true, I would never have been born. Does that make sense?"

An's first impulse was to tell Eden these were only dreams. She had obviously been born, and even though she knew nothing about her past, she was here now. But he thought better of it; Eden had warned him there was more she needed to say.

"It does, Eden, if it happened as you've described it in your dream. But I think you have more to tell me, don't you?"

Eden was pleased that he remembered her asking him to wait to respond until after she had finished speaking.

"Once inside, Other Worlds is just a large room with blank white walls, nothing on them, no windows or doors, no people other than Raymond, Shelly..." She paused again, staring intently at An, watching for a reaction to what she was about to say, "...and an Asian man named Giáp."

An looked out across the water below them while listening to Eden. Hearing this, he showed no outward emotion. He knew why Eden found this so difficult to say.

She continued.

"Your father's name, An. I know you know that. I also know 'Giáp' is a fairly common Vietnamese name. I could have dreamed his name because of what your mother told me, but I didn't dream it after meeting her or you. I had before we met. All of it, about Raymond and Shelly, Other Worlds, and Giáp: he's not there randomly, An. In some way, he is the reason Shelly and Raymond are there, and me now as well. If this had only felt like a dream, as it did initially, I wouldn't be telling you this now." She reached up to gently touch An's face, turning his head toward her, her eyes locking onto his.

"It is, real, An, every bit of it."

Without saying it aloud, both knew it was best to let Eden's words settle.

Eden knows I might doubt everything she said, including her sanity. I do, to some degree. But that's just a quick judgment; I owe it to her and our relationship to ask questions.

"Eden, I need to think about this before responding. There are many questions I should ask you, but right now, I don't know what they are. However, I want you to know I take what you've told me seriously. I know you are not making this up; you are troubled, searching for answers. I want to help you find what you need to know. If being in Singapore is causing these dreams and discomfort, we will go somewhere else. Is there anything else you feel I should know or that you want to ask of me?"

"Thank you, An, for listening and for convincing me you are seriously considering what I've said. I assumed you would, but it means a lot to hear you say it. I do have one more request of you."

"What is it, Eden? I will do whatever I can."

"If you dream anything related to what I've told you, please share it with me. We can only work through whatever is happening to me if each of us shares everything we think or dream, some of which might provide answers."

"I will, Eden."

The rest of their visit to the Chinese Garden went well, helped by both of them trying to show the other that whatever was bothering Eden would soon be identified and corrected. But that was more a façade than reality. An knew she was troubled. Increasingly, he was as well. As yet, he had no dreams, but his thoughts while awake were revealing cracks in his certainty that her dreams were just that—only dreams.

CHAPTER FORTY-FOUR

Life for both Eden and An continued much as it had before their day off visiting the Chinese Garden. They traveled around Singapore looking for sites An would photograph, which Eden agreed were good subjects for her pencil drawings. The concept was working both artistically and financially. While they still sold individual works separately, they sold more when pairing An's photos with Eden's drawings.

Linh was doing an excellent job managing all back-office tasks. Since she was based in Vietnam, they also discovered a tax benefit they hadn't anticipated. Linh transferred money to Eden's and An's joint account for all customer shipments. This lowered their tax liability compared to sales processed in Singapore, and in the future, wherever they establish their artist residencies. However, this did require one or both of them to return to Vietnam at least once a year to personally sign their Vietnamese company tax returns. The government would accept Linh's review and signature for the mandatory quarterly reports, but only An's or Eden's for the end-of-year filings.

This was not a problem for either of them, since Singapore was a little more than two hours from Vietnam by plane. How they would handle it when they moved their residence farther away would be decided later. In the meantime, Eden, An, and certainly Linh were happy that one or both of them could spend more time with her while following government rules. An would be the first to do so, while Eden remained in Singapore, working.

Stepping off the Reunification Express train in Da Nang, An thought about how fortunate he and his mother were to spend a week together while meeting with their accountant to review their tax filing. But he had something else he planned to discuss with her as well. Although he hadn't mentioned anything to Eden shortly after their visit to the Chinese Garden, or since, he had experienced in Singapore something similar to the dreams Eden told him she was having. Not about Raymond and Shelly, but one involving a stranger. A man who befriended him during a search for one of his photo sites. He wasn't sure what he would say to his mother. The connection to Eden's dreams was at best weak. The third man in her dreams was Asian, just like the stranger who approached him at Làng Nướng Vietnamese restaurant.

An and Linh spent the first two days of their visit meeting with their accountant. Afterwards, they went to the local tax authority so An could verify and sign the filing in person, as required by law. With the business side now complete, An looked forward to a quiet visit with his mother, during which he planned to bring up the stranger who had approached him in Singapore.

"I know returning to Vietnam for tax matters is an inconvenience for you, An, but I genuinely look forward to seeing you and Eden. Hopefully, she can join you next time."

"She told me to tell you she will come next time, with or without me. Someone has to stay home and work."

"That's good to hear; I so enjoyed meeting and talking with her on your first visit."

"Mother, I have something I want to talk to you about. Can we do that now?"

"Certainly, An, whatever you like."

"You've told me something about my father. I don't recall asking many questions, but I do have a few now if you don't mind."

Linh wondered what An would ask her, but she quickly reminded herself that he was now a young man. He had a right to learn as much as he could about his father. She would answer as honestly as possible.

"You told me he was forced to fight for the North; if he refused, they would have killed him and his entire family, including you. Is that right?"

Now that she knew the subject would be Giáp, and having promised herself she would hold nothing back, she answered.

"It is. The Vietcong executed men who resisted recruitment as soldiers. In some cases, they first killed their family members in front of them before executing those who refused to join. They ordered neighbors to witness these killings as a warning. I saw some of this firsthand. It was horrible. I cannot erase it from my mind all these years later."

He saw his mother struggling to explain what had happened and briefly thought he shouldn't ask any more about his father.

But what I want to know is about the stranger who approached me in Singapore—that, and maybe what she thinks of Eden's dreams. First, I will focus on the stranger, and depending on how that goes, I may bring up her dreams afterward.

"I don't mean to upset you or force you to recall that horrible time. I apologize."

Linh regained her composure.

"It's okay, An. The past is part of you and me. You have a right to know everything I know. What else can I tell you?"

"Thank you, Mother. I was doing a photo shoot in Singapore a couple of weeks ago and stopped for lunch at a Vietnamese restaurant, one of the oldest outside Vietnam. It was crowded, but there was room at my table. An Asian man approached and asked if I minded him having lunch at my table, since no other tables were available. I welcomed him, and he sat down. We spoke briefly after the server left with our orders. He asked if I was Vietnamese. It wasn't an unusual question; I wondered the same about him, since we were both Asian, eating in a well-known, highly regarded Vietnamese restaurant. He was about your age, Mother, old enough to have experienced the war years as an adult. I asked him where he had lived during the war. He mentioned Hội An, Quảng Nam Province, as if I hadn't heard of it. I told him I was raised there, but I was a baby for most of the war and had little memory of that time. I was going to ask if he had been a soldier in the war and, if so, on which side. But I decided that would be too much to ask of a stranger."

He paused, silently recognizing that he was making no progress toward asking his mother what he wanted to know. Linh did, too.

"You said you wanted to ask me a question, maybe more than one. Your lunch with this stranger is interesting, but you haven't asked me anything except whether your father was forced to fight for the North. I told you he was. Is there anything else you would like to know?"

An knew he could not fool his mother. He would either ask more questions or drop the subject. He decided to continue.

"Do you ever dream of Father?"

"I do, quite often."

"Can you tell me what you dream?"

"His body might be dead. I've never known what truly happened to him. If so, he is no longer on this earth; his body returns to the earth, while his soul moves to another place or realm. We are Buddhists, An. We don't die as other believers perceive death. We move through realms seeking to reach nirvana. Although I cannot be certain, after all this time, I believe your father's mortal life ended long ago. If that is so, his soul continues, traveling through different realms of existence. In my dreams, he lives to attain nirvana. To do so, he must guide those of us left behind, protect us, and help us live our best lives."

"Does he speak to you in your dreams?"

"Not as you are doing to me now. But I feel his presence. I have questions for you, An."

"What are they, Mother?"

"Do you dream of the father you never knew? If so, does he speak to you? If he does, what does he say?"

An knew his mother had just redirected their conversation from her to him.

“I'm not sure, but—,” he paused, unsure whether to finish the thought, fearing it would upset his mother.

“An, just as I should not hold back anything from you, you should tell me everything. I want to help you.”

“I might have recently, Mother. I wondered if the Vietnamese stranger I had lunch with might be the reincarnation of my father.”

"If you substitute 'rebirth' for 'reincarnation,' the Buddhist interpretation, it is possible. If it were him, how would you feel about that?"

“I don’t know, which is why I wanted to talk to you. What do you think?”

"I often feel your father's presence. He is not lost to me; he exists in another realm, another time. I hope to join him. That stranger could be your father in ways you, as a mortal, cannot understand. He could be reaching out to help you. However, be very careful deciding who is and is not him; many might try to deceive you for their own gain. Is there anything more you would like to ask?"

"Not at this moment. You have given me much to consider. But I will not hesitate to ask you more if I feel it necessary. Thank you, Mother."

CHAPTER FORTY-FIVE

It is time for you to come, An.

Time for what?

For answers to your questions, no one else can answer.

Friday morning marked the start of another three-day weekend. The time when An and Eden achieved their greatest sales. On any other Friday morning, An would look forward to the three days that followed. He enjoyed meeting and talking with those interested in the art he and Eden had produced separately and together.

Today was different; his mind was elsewhere, struggling to make sense of what Shelly and his mother had told him. Recently, he was almost sure he repeatedly saw the Vietnamese stranger he had shared a table with at lunch. Not approaching or talking to him, only glimpses of him, or someone who looked like him, in the crowds, moving through areas where he and Eden displayed their art. Today, the Raffles Hotel, a favorite spot for international tourists.

"An, are you feeling okay? You don't seem as enthusiastic as you usually are, especially at the start of the weekend."

An looked away from the crowd to answer Eden.

"I'm sorry, what did you say?"

"I asked if you are feeling okay?"

"Oh, yes, you did. I'm fine, just a little tired," he said, hoping Eden would accept his answer and ask no more questions.

Eden finished assembling her display of their art. The morning was still early. The larger crowds would not come until late morning through late afternoon, when they would head back to their hotels, Eden hoped, carrying the art they had purchased from her.

Edin did not fully accept his tiredness as an explanation for not doing his part in their setup. Usually, he would have completed it before Eden finished her tasks. Today, he seemed more focused on watching the crowd as if he were looking for someone.

"An, I'm going for coffee. Can I bring you something?"

Still distracted, An did not respond.

"An! I said I am going for coffee and I'll bring it back. Is there anything you would like me to bring you?"

Her voice, louder the second time, drew An's attention.

"I'm sorry, Eden. You're going for coffee, yes, that would be nice. My usual," he said, now appearing to give his full attention to setting up to sell, hoping Eden would think everything was normal.

But it wasn't for An. He was sure he was seeing the Vietnamese man he had lunch with a few weeks earlier. Not clearly, just flashes of him in the crowd, always as if he were looking in his direction.

Is he looking for me? For what reason? If that is him, he can see me. Why doesn't he come over to talk to me? What does he want?

Now, An, come now!

CHAPTER FORTY-SIX

"WELL, HELLO! AN, ISN'T IT?"

An missed seeing the man approach until he was standing in front of him. Startled, he stumbled in response.

"Ah, yes, I am."

"You don't remember me, An? We shared a lunch table at Làng Nướng a few weeks ago. My name is Giáp," he said, his hand outstretched for An to shake.

"Yes, of course, I recall now. Are you just passing by on your way somewhere?"

"You could say so. I saw you and the young woman who was here a few minutes ago setting up your artwork. I recalled our lunch meeting. You mentioned you were an artist, and now, this morning, seeing you with all your creations, I see that you are," he said, looking at what was already in place, with much more still to be displayed.

This all makes sense, but I don't recall saying what I do for a living. I must have, or else how would he know?

"Thank you for the compliment," An replied, glancing around at what was left to do, hoping the stranger would take the hint and leave. When he didn't, An's curiosity about him grew, and he decided to take the lead in the conversation.

"Forgive me. If you told me your name at lunch, I've forgotten it. I apologize."

The stranger laughed. "Memories are funny things, aren't they? Full of so much useless information, we can't recall what we're looking for. My name is Giáp."

What does he want from me?

"I have to be going, An, but it is good to see you again, and I wish you and your partner great sales success today. And just so you do not forget my name the next time we meet," he said, smiling, "...here's my business card. You and your partner should drop by when you have time."

An accepted the card without looking at it, placing it in his shirt pocket as the two of them shook hands.

"Thank you, Giáp, maybe we will."

Eden soon returned with two cups of coffee and handed one to An.

"I can see you didn't get much done. Are you sure you're feeling okay? If not, take the day off. I can handle it here alone if you take some of this that isn't yet on display back with you."

"I'm fine. Shortly after you left, someone approached me to talk about our art. I couldn't continue setting up while he was here; it would have been rude. He just left a few minutes before you returned."

An purposely chose not to tell Eden who that someone was. There was still too much left to do, and Eden would ask too many questions he could not answer. He would tell her who the stranger was and what he meant to him, just not now.

Later that night, back in the apartment, very tired but happy with the sales they had achieved, An reflected on what they had accomplished and what he hoped would happen on Saturday and Sunday.

We're off to an excellent start to the weekend, with most of it our combined pencil-and-photography art. Together, the two of us sell significantly more than either does alone, at higher prices. But I'm very tired. It's so good to be home, in bed.

CHAPTER FORTY-SEVEN

An awoke the next morning as tired as he had been when he went to bed. Even more so, thinking about the day ahead, with another to follow on Sunday. He could hear noises from the kitchen and assumed it was Eden preparing breakfast.

Tired or not, it's time to get up and get ready.

It was then that he remembered a dream so vivid, he could see it clearly in his mind, beginning with a voice speaking to him.

Follow the light, An.

I see the light, very dim, now getting brighter. Where will it take me?

To answer questions you hadn't known to ask. Come now, An.

What is this place?

An looked around, seeing nothing he recognized. He could hear traffic passing on an elevated road above him. The area around him appeared commercial, with the type of buildings one would find in low-rent industrial areas. Nothing like anything he was familiar with in Singapore, Barcelona, or Vietnam. No one was around to tell him where he was. He had no idea what to do.

"Hello, An. I'm happy you came."

An turned to see a middle-aged Asian man standing directly

behind him, smiling. He looked vaguely familiar, as if he might have known him at some point in the past, though he had no idea where.

"Good, someone I can ask for help. I have no idea where I am. Can you tell me?"

Still smiling, the Asian man responded. "I will, but first check in your shirt pocket."

He did as the man directed, pulling out a business card. On it, he read, "Đoàn ăn Giáp, Other Worlds Coffee."

Looking back at the man, he wasn't sure what to say or do.

"Let me help you, An. Follow me. I will buy you a coffee unlike any you've had before," he said, turning and motioning for An to follow him.

Less than twenty steps away, An looked up at a sign atop a building he hadn't noticed before. He hesitated as a pinpoint of bright light at the center of the now-open door grew larger and more colorful as he approached. Unafraid, he stepped through into Other Worlds.

Once inside, the door shut behind him, and the light went out. He felt his body suspended, floating. The building's interior walls were a white, fluid, translucent spiral, reflecting fragments of incomplete images that floated in and out around him. Images of his mother, of himself as a child, a growing boy, and, more recently, a young man. Along with them, fragments of an image of a Vietnamese man. All this, and himself, floated toward the center of a vortex, drawing them all closer—to what, An did not know.

The deeper he went into the vortex, the faster an unknown force pulled him along. There was no escaping its power, and now, along with it, a low-frequency hum he had not initially heard grew in pitch and volume, seemingly pushing him further and further.

Finally, the hum faded away, and everything was dark. He could see nothing in the blackness. He heard and felt the shock of what he thought was thunder striking nearby. Slowly opening his tightly shut eyes, he found he was in a room with no windows or doors. White walls, ceiling, and floor, each melting into the other with no apparent separation, as though he were inside a globe. Nothing else was visible; he was sitting in an overstuffed leather chair, with a small table beside it holding a cup of hot coffee, steam rising.

Welcome to Other Worlds, An.

A voice in his head, the words not spoken by anyone, he was alone.

"You have questions."

He turned toward a now-clear voice. There, sitting directly across from him, were the Vietnamese man he had come to know as Giáp, a man and a woman he did not know, and Eden.

CHAPTER FORTY-EIGHT

NO ONE SPOKE. GIÁP, RAYMOND, SHELLY, AND EDEN SAT ON ONE SIDE, facing An alone, opposite them. Thoughts but no words passed between them until An spoke.

"Why am I here?"

"For answers to questions you haven't known to ask."

"Who are you?"

"My name is Đoàn ăn Giáp. Would you like to know more about me?"

"I have no choice, do I?"

"You do, An. If you choose not to learn more, you will return to life as you remember it. You won't recall Other Worlds, me, Raymond Quinn, or Shelly Bennett. You will know Eden only as she was before this moment. She will remember you only as she did before. But understand this: that life will include the frustrations you both had before, especially you, An. She chose to be here, agreeing to continue her journey and seeking answers to questions she hadn't known to ask. Now, you must decide what you will do."

"Eden and I will be together as we were if I do not ask questions?"

"Yes."

An turned to face Eden.

"What do you want me to do?"

"That is not for me to decide. What I want has nothing to do with you deciding what you want or will do. Only you can decide that, An."

He looked back at Giáp.

"You asked if I was ready to learn more about you. Why would I do that instead of first learning more about Eden or these two?" he said, motioning toward Shelly and Raymond.

"That is yours to decide as well; however, you need to learn more about me to understand yourself better and find answers to all your questions."

An attempted to stand up quickly, realizing he couldn't. Something prevented him from moving. He felt a sense of calm wash over him, like a warm fog blanket on a dark night. He believed that what he should do would become clear if he said and did nothing.

Hours passed without anyone speaking or exchanging unspoken thoughts. To An, a split second to decide what he would do. First looking at Giáp, then at Raymond, Shelly, and finally at Eden for a longer moment, he turned back to Giáp to speak.

"I choose to stay, starting with you, Giáp. What do you want me to know?"

"Much more than you will learn here in our brief time together. But it will be the start of your journey, one you will undertake with Eden as she shares hers with you."

Giáp, now standing, moved to his left, turning away from An, before continuing.

"I was in your life, the father you never knew. I still am while searching for my place in the multiverse. I was and still am your mother's husband. We were and still are your parents. I was killed in the Chiến tranh Việt Nam. This man," he motioned to Raymond, sitting next to him, "killed me the same moment I killed him."

Giáp paused to let An process what he had just heard—his face showing shock and confusion. Once again, no one said anything for a split second, which felt like an eternity.

No longer restrained, An stood up, now able to move freely.

"You are my father. You are dead. This man is dead. If true, which I doubt, what does that have to do with Eden?"

"Everything you hear from the four of us is the truth. We are unable to tell you anything that is not true. Accept that, and you will quickly learn what you want to know."

An turned and walked behind his chair, his back to the others. "Everything is true, is it?" He turned again to face them. "Okay, I believe you. Now tell me, what does what you have said so far have to do with Eden?"

"The answers to your questions must follow the same order as the events that brought us here. That starts with you and me. I would have been there for you as you grew up if Raymond Quinn and I hadn't killed each other in battle. Your mother, my wife, was pregnant with you at the time. You were born, and she raised you without me there as your father."

An turned to look at Raymond.

"You killed my father; he killed you. Not much I can blame you for in that, is there?"

Raymond replied, "You are free to blame me for whatever you wish. What I deserve to be blamed for is another matter."

"Okay, what do you and my father dying in the war have to do with this woman next to you and with Eden?"

Shelly responded.

"Raymond and I wrote to each other while he was in Vietnam and I was in Zimbabwe. We were falling in love and planned to meet in Singapore while he was away from the war. I went, he didn't, and I heard nothing more from or about him. I was devastated and took my own life five years after his death. Since then, I have learned that we would have been married if neither of us had died."

"You are dead. The man you were going to marry is dead—killed by my father, whom he killed. It just keeps getting better and better, doesn't it? Next, one of you will tell me she's dead," he said, looking at and gesturing toward Eden. "I don't need to hear anything more."

Giáp responded quickly.

"You do, much more, and when you have heard it all, you and the four of us must decide what to do. You do not understand what Eden has to do with any of this; you only make sarcastic remarks, even though you don't believe what we tell you. However, let's discuss Eden's role in all this. Better yet, sit down and let Eden tell you herself."

CHAPTER FORTY-NINE

An sat down, his mind clouded with equal parts fear, anger, and uncertainty. His feelings for Eden compelled him to stay.

Eden stood up, walking the short distance from her chair to An's.

"I hope you will listen; it's important for both of us that you do. I realize you are confused; I was, too, when I learned about my situation. I wish I could explain how all of this came to be. I can't. I only know that this is our reality now. We have all been forced to make a choice. We have made our decisions; you must as well. You can choose to join us as we try to understand what our eternal futures will be. If you decide not to, you will go back to the life you were living before we met. What will you do, An?"

Surprised by Eden's abrupt explanation of what was happening to him. He waited for her to say more, and when she didn't, he replied.

"Eden, you do know how much of a shock this is for me, don't you?"

"I do, An, just as it was for me and the others. You have questions. We all do. But there are no answers. We all had to make the same choice you are now forced to make. You can return to your life as it was before we met. If you decide that is what you want to do, you will have no recollection of where you are now, of Raymond, Shelly, or me. You will know you had a father," she said, her head turning slightly toward Giáp. "But nothing more about him. It is time for you to choose, An. What do you want to do?"

An looked at the others. No one said anything. He stood, turning his back on all of them and walking a few steps away as if he would leave. He saw no doors or windows, only the white walls fading into the equally white floor and ceiling. He was once again inside a globe that began to swirl, forming a pinpoint at the start of a vortex.

Is that how I would leave?

Eden replied, "Yes, and for eternity if that is your choice."

He turned back to face Giáp, Raymond, Shelly, and Eden, saying nothing, his thoughts making his confusion clear.

"An, I am your father. I was not there for you when you were growing up, but I am here now, when you need me even more. I cannot tell you what to do. I can only emphasize that you must decide, accepting the consequences of your choice for all eternity. If you choose to stay with us, you will forfeit the rest of your mortal life before meeting Eden. We don't know what that would be; neither do you. The only way to find out is to experience it. If you decide to join us, you will search for a life you would have lived had you made different choices. One of your infinite unlived lives."

"Your father is telling you the truth, An. I cannot tell you what to do, but I can explain how and why I made my decision. Maybe what you hear will help you decide what is best for you," Eden said, returning to her seat.

"I chose love for these souls I am connected to because of events and outcomes I did *not* choose. For me, there was no other option. My soul was lost in the multiverse. Once I realized this, my choices became clear: leave this place and these souls, who exist throughout eternity, or join them in searching for my eternity while helping them find theirs. For them and me, there really wasn't any other alternative. But there is for you. We are all dead or never born. You were born; you can return to that life if you choose to."

An looked at Eden and the others silently. More time passed—seconds, minutes, hours—no one in Other Worlds knew or cared as they waited for his decision. Though his heart had been full of indecision just moments before, he now knew exactly what he would choose.

"Our lifetimes do not begin and end with mortal birth and death. We existed in the multiverse before beginning our mortal lives and continue to do so after they end. The decisions we make during that liminal time prepare us to make choices like those facing me now. I choose love for all of you and accept your love for me. I choose, for all eternity, to help you in your search for your eternal lives, and I accept your help in finding mine."

Giáp stood up, taking a step towards An.

"You have chosen what I hoped for but could not ask of you. We are grateful you have decided to stay with us. Each of us must now seek resolution. We believed we were doomed to struggle through mortal and immortal lives alone as lost souls. Separate journeys, now all of us together. As you will learn, I did not abandon you, An. I need your help finding my way back. You need my help finding your way forward. We will help each other. Raymond, Shelly, you both must start from where your lives would have been if your mortal lives hadn't ended when and how they did. You and I would have survived the war, Raymond. You would have returned to Vietnam after your R&R with Shelly, and when your war tour was over, you would have left the army and begun your adult life in Seattle. You would not have committed suicide, Shelly. You and Raymond would have communicated through letters, planning for you to join him in Seattle. Think about what that would have been like for both of you, as well as what it now means for your eternal journey."

Giáp moved to Eden and stood before her.

"Your parents will not have died; you would be born. You must work through feelings as if you had been left to find your way on your own. You will experience mortal life with An once he and I have resolved our issues. When that is done, he will be in a position to help you."

"Giáp, is visiting what appears to be more of our unlived lives all we need to do?" Raymond asked, as if he knew the answer to his question.

"No, it isn't, Raymond. You and I will address that when the right moment comes."

CHAPTER FIFTY

THE TWO-AND-A-HALF-TON TRUCK PULLED OVER TO THE SIDE OF THE ROAD leading into Hội An, stopping just long enough for Giáp to climb down from the back. His few belongings were wrapped in a small bag slung over his shoulder, with a rope tied from one side to the other, forming a loop. He was exhausted from the more than six-hour ride from the reeducation camp he had been released from in An Khe earlier that morning. There was no water to wash the dust from his nose, mouth, and eyes, which swirled into the open truck bed where he and other recently released prisoners were riding before being dropped off close to—but not at—their homes. Forced to walk the rest of the way, Giáp looked around, seeing little he remembered before being conscripted into an NVA unit to fight against the South Vietnamese and Americans years earlier. He could have refused had he been willing to watch his pregnant wife murdered in front of him, followed by his own death. How long ago that was, he could not recall. His mind and memories were crushed by years of brutal internment by the communists now running Vietnam.

He hoped his wife, Linh, would still be at the thatched-roof hut on stilts they had shared before he was forced to leave. He quickened his pace the last mile of a multiyear involuntary journey through constant pain, deprivation, and beatings, witnessing death repeatedly, now almost over.

I wonder if she still looks the same. I know I don't.

The farther he walked into and through Hội An, the more it felt like home. Both sides spared Hội An from destruction. There was some damage, but most of it had been cleaned up and repaired while he spent years in a re-education prison for a crime he did not commit.

Rounding the final bend in the dirt road, he would reach his home, assuming it was still a place he could call his own.

Oh, thank God, it is there! I would recognize it anywhere.

In the distance in front of the hut, he saw a young boy.

Linh was pregnant when the Vietcong forced me to go with them. That was at least ten years ago, maybe longer. Could that be my son?

No longer feeling tired or in pain, he quickened his pace until he was just a few meters from the boy.

"Excuse me," he said, prompting the boy, who looked to be ten or twelve years old and slightly tall for his age, to turn around.

He looks like I did when I was his age. That is my son!

The boy looked up at Giáp but did not respond.

Giáp decided it was best not to reveal himself. That could wait; he just wanted to ensure the boy lived here with his mother.

"I'm sorry, I'm so dirty; I've come a long way. Do you live here?" Giáp said, gesturing to the hut behind the boy.

"Yes, with my grandmother."

He didn't mention his mother. I pray she's all right.

Having heard a conversation outside, the boy's grandmother stepped out of the hut to see who was speaking with her grandson. She did not recognize Giáp, but he immediately recognized her as Linh's mother.

"What do you want? There's nothing here for you to steal. We don't have enough for the two of us."

I always called her Bà nội. If she is the boy's grandmother, she will remember, even if she doesn't recognize me.

"Bà nơi, là cháu, Giáp đây. Cháu đã về nhà rồi."

Her expression, a combination of fear and sternness just moments before, now became recognition of her son-in-law, whom she had long believed was dead.

Almost in a whisper, she spoke. "Giáp, is that really you?"

"Yes, it is, Bà nơi, I've finally been allowed to come home."

Hearing this and studying Giáp's face more closely, she realized the thin, dirty stranger was her son-in-law, whom she believed had been killed in the war over ten years ago.

"I thought you were dead, Linh thought you were dead. We heard nothing from or about you. Where have you been? Please come in; you look so tired. An, bring your father some water to drink."

An's head snapped around to look at this stranger, whom he had just been told was his father.

My father! How can that be? Mother told me he was dead, killed in the war.

Giáp followed his mother-in-law's instructions, climbing the steps and entering the hut he had built for Linh years earlier. His eyes scanned the area, noting things he did not recognize alongside others he did, including what had been his chair. He wanted to sit in it, but he waited for grandmother to tell him where she preferred him to sit.

"Please, Giáp, sit in your chair. An, bring water for your father."

An emerged from a room Giáp remembered as the place where they prepared food. He accepted the cup of water An offered, thanked him, and took a sip.

"That is so good, thank you, Bà nơi, and you, An. That is your name, isn't it?"

An nodded, still not saying anything, continuing to stare at Giáp as though he were a ghost.

Anticipating the worst, Giáp looked back at An's grandmother and, almost in a whisper, asked, "Is Linh home?" She looked away from Giáp before answering.

"You don't know. You couldn't have. Linh died two years ago. She had been sick for a long time and finally passed. I've been living here ever since, taking care of An. Although more and more, he takes care of me," she said, looking at An. "I'm sorry, Giáp. I know you loved Linh very much, as she did you."

Giáp did not respond right away. His head tilted toward the floor, trying not to let Grandmother or An see his tears just starting to streak through the dust on his cheeks, leaving tracks as if they had flowed from muddy water.

"I feared she would not be here, that she would be..." he paused again, unable to finish the thought.

He hadn't known what to expect, but learning that Linh was dead was still a shock. He told himself she would survive the war, the threat of death, whether accidental or intentional, coming from either side. She would not die.

"If you are my father, why did you go away? Why weren't you with Mother and me? We needed you," An suddenly asked, his first words since Giáp arrived home.

"An, that is disrespectful. Do not speak to your father that way."

"That's okay, Bà nơi. He doesn't know, and he has a right to ask."

Turning to An, he asked, "How old are you, son?"

"Ten."

"You must have been born shortly after I was taken away. Your mother was still pregnant with you then."

An responded, "Taken away? Who took you, and where did you go?'

"The Vietcong ordered me to fight against the South Vietnamese and Americans. They said if I did not, they would kill your mother with you in her, not yet born, while I was forced to watch. And when she was dead, they would kill me. I had no choice but to go with them, to do as they said. I did so for three years until the war ended."

"Why didn't you come home then?"

"Thousands of others and I were placed in forced labor prison camps. The communists called them re-education camps to indoctrinate us into communism. I've been in one near An Khe for the last seven years. I was released early this morning. Others and I rode all day in the back of an open truck, and I was let off a couple of kilometers from here a few hours ago."

An did not respond, his eyes shifted from staring at Giáp to looking down at the floor.

"An, I couldn't be with you, your mother, and Bà Nơi. They would have killed us all, as they did others. But I am here now. If you or Bà Nơi want me to go," he paused, looking at Grandmother, "I will. I want to stay with you. That is why I came back, but it is up to you and Bà Nơi."

"Please do stay as long as you like, Giáp. I need your help. An needs his father. I will move my things out of your room. I moved in there after Linh passed. You can clean up. I know you're tired. I will fix you something to eat."

"Thank you, Bà nơi, but there is no need for you to move. I will sleep in the small room. It will feel huge compared with how I slept in prison. I do want to clean up, and I am hungry. I will take care of that now. Thank you both," he said, looking back at An, who was once again looking down at the floor to avoid eye contact with his father.

Grandmother and Giáp talked during dinner mostly about Linh's illness, with Giáp briefly answering Grandmother's few questions about life in the forced labor camp. She could see he wasn't comfortable discussing it more than necessary.

Dinner now done, Giáp helped Grandmother clean and put away the dishes. Afterwards, he hugged her, wished her good sleep, and looked for An to say goodnight.

"I'm going to bed now, An. I hope you sleep well."

An did not look up from his book, merely nodding. Giáp could not tell whether he was actually reading or just avoiding eye contact. He decided not to press it.

A shocking day for all of us, but much worse when you are ten years old and meet a stranger who claims to be your father. We will work on it together.

Giáp quickly fell into a deep sleep, dreaming he was back in the prison camp with guards screaming at him and other prisoners, beating the backs of their legs with bamboo rods. Hard enough to leave large reddish-brown bruises, not hard enough to break the skin.

Three a.m. came, and he awoke, still very tired. Time to get up in the camp and start work.

It will take time for me to adjust to this new life.

CHAPTER FIFTY-ONE

LIFE FOR GIÁP IMPROVED GREATLY COMPARED WITH HIS TIME IN THE RE-education prison camp, where he often thought death was a better option. He soon found work in the Tra Que vegetable fields as a farm laborer, removing weeds, trimming plants, harvesting, digging irrigation canals, and bringing fresh water from nearby streams to the fields. Every morning, six days a week, he walked forty-five minutes from his home, crossing Nguyễn Trường Tộ and Đ. Hai Bà Trưng Road to get to work, arriving before everyone else and staying until the last worker left. The farm owner recognized his value and promoted him to oversee all the field workers. Now earning more money, he was able to do more for An and Bà nơi. However, his relationship with An remained his greatest concern.

Telling him I am his father and that I want to be here to protect him and his mother means little to him. He only knows what I haven't done. But he will understand in time. I will work hard to improve his life, and he will recognize and appreciate what I do for him and his grandmother.

Most evenings, Giáp would clean up after coming home from work, have dinner with Grandmother and An, helping her with any chores she was too tired to do during the day. Then he would relax in his chair, sometimes falling asleep before Grandmother woke him to go to bed.

Don't give up, Giáp. An needs you and will soon accept you as his father.

But will he ever forgive me for not being here to protect you and him? I pray he will, Linh, but sometimes I wonder if it will ever happen. Maybe I was wrong to stay here after discovering you had passed.

And what would have become of Bà nơi had you not stayed? What would have become of An, only ten years old when you returned?

Oh, Linh, I miss you so much.

Giáp had been home for three years, a period that passed quickly for him. His role at the Tra Que farm grew increasingly important as he assumed greater responsibilities, and his salary rose, enabling him to support An and his grandmother. While she continued her chores around the house, she no longer had to take in laundry or mend clothes for others. She finally had time to rest, which made Giáp very proud. More than that, An, now a teenager, began to see his father differently. He realized his father had always cared for him and his mother, and that he would never have left had he not been forced to. An understood that was why he was still alive today. He wanted to learn more about his father but wasn't sure how to approach him with his many questions. In the end, he decided to begin by apologizing for his behavior since Giáp's return three years earlier.

Like all previous Saturday afternoons since he started working at the Tra Que farm, Giáp was at home, done for the day, relaxing in his chair after dinner, looking forward to Sunday, his only day off.

"Father, may I talk with you?"

Though not asleep, Giáp had closed his eyes, thinking about what he might do the next day. Hearing An's voice, he opened his eyes and replied.

"Certainly, An, anything you want."

An sat in a chair across from his father, now unsure how to say what only moments before he thought would come easily. He hesitated, looking exactly like Giáp knew him to be, an awkward teenage boy.

"Father, I... I apologize for how I have treated you since you returned. I was angry at you for not being here with me, Bà nơi, and Mother before she passed. You told me why you couldn't be." He hesitated again, looking down at the floor. Knowing what to say but feeling embarrassed, he continued. "Mother told me many times. You did not want to leave, but you did to save our lives. The Vietcong would have killed us, and you, if you refused to go with them to fight their enemy. I am so sorry for how I have treated you, Father. Please forgive me."

Hearing this, Giáp, now fully awake, realized it was a pivotal moment in their relationship. Since his release from the prison camp three years ago, he had wondered whether An would ever accept him as his father. Would he ever understand the reason for his absence during the ten years since An's birth? And now it had become clear. Giáp knew that An saying what he did was extremely difficult for him. He admitted he was wrong about something he was sure was true. Giáp understood he now needed to be even more careful how he responded.

"Thank you for telling me this, An. I understand it hasn't been easy for you to share, and even harder to admit to yourself. If you accept everything I've said since I re-entered your life three years ago, please accept what I say now. You are my son. I loved you and your mother when I was forced to leave before you were born. I have loved both of you just as much in the three years since I returned. But now, based on what you've told me tonight, my love for you, your mother, and Bà nơi is complete and eternal. Thank you, An."

CHAPTER FIFTY-TWO

AN RECOGNIZING HIM AS HIS FATHER, UNDERSTANDING WHY HE COULDN'T be with him and his mother when An was born meant everything to Giáp. Life was better than either of them had expected after their conversation five years earlier. There were challenges, and none greater than the night Bà nơi passed quietly in her sleep.

Giáp arranged for her ashes to be placed next to Linh's. Giáp and An preferred a small Buddhist service attended by only a few close friends, some of whom knew Linh, along with elderly friends of Bà nơi. Now, at the end of the Buddhist mourning period, Giáp and An sat at a table, their food before them, neither eating much. Looking down at his now-cold bowl of soup, Giáp stirred it absentmindedly, as if it were still too hot. He spoke.

"I think there must be more we should have done to honor Bà nơi."

An looked up from his uneaten dinner, surprised to hear this from his father.

"We followed most of the Buddhist traditions, certainly the ones Bà nơi said were important to her. Many of her friends were there and expressed their sorrow at her passing. What more do you think we should have done, Father?"

"I don't know. Maybe nothing. Maybe what I'm feeling has nothing to do with her passing or her funeral. Something is bothering me, but I can't say what it is."

You know, Giáp. Open your eyes, talk to me.

Giáp did as the voice instructed, realizing he was back in Other Worlds, alone with Raymond Quinn, seated in leather chairs facing each other. No one else was in the room.

"Strange, isn't it, Raymond? I call others to join me here to help them, but not this time. You called me. Why? Because you need me to answer more of your questions?"

"With one exception, no."

"What exception?"

"To ask why you haven't called *me* here so we can finally do what we've never done before."

"I believe I know what you mean, but tell me anyway."

"At first, you were Asian, or at least that's how I referred to you. Then you revealed yourself to be Đoàn ăn Giáp, a soldier fighting for the North. You later corrected that, saying you were a *conscripted* soldier forced to fight for the North, adding that both you and your family would be killed if you refused. You told Shelly you were her conscience, forcing her to confront what she would prefer to ignore. *I've* called *you* here to compel you to do what you must to find that 'forever' you are searching for. And, as you told An, that process must start at the beginning with you and me."

Giáp knew what Raymond was referring to. They were long overdue trying to discover the point of each simultaneously killing the other.

CHAPTER FIFTY-THREE

GIÁP STOOD FROM HIS CHAIR, HOPING TO APPEAR DEFIANT TO MASK HIS fear. He expected and welcomed this reckoning between Raymond and himself, but now that it was here... He began by challenging Raymond to answer questions he did not know how to answer.

"We killed each other, you believing you were helping the oppressed. You saw me as your enemy. You didn't know that my wife, our soon-to-be-born son, and I were the ones you wished to protect. We both met a violent end, Raymond, but here we are together now. What are we searching for?"

Raymond paused, looking for an answer to Giáp's question. There had to be a reason.

"Ever since you forced me to accept my death, later telling me it was at your hands, I considered it the end. My life ended the same split second yours did. That could not be a mere coincidence. Giáp, what if that was the beginning, not the end? If so, maybe understanding the reason for our deaths requires us to see them as necessary before we can begin searching the multiverse for our eternal lives."

Giáp looked directly at Raymond before responding.

"Our deaths were not just the start of our search; they marked the beginning of reconciliation among all our unlived lives. You, me, Shelly, An, Eden, and countless others yet to be born. We were not connected before our deaths, but in our eternal lives in the multiverse, we are. What does that mean? What do we do, and what do we tell others to do?"

Raymond paused for a moment, wanting to respond meaningfully. He wasn't sure either of them could be certain what that would be, but he had more to say.

"It means we've all been viewing life and death incorrectly, and none more so than you and me. We didn't just want to understand why we died, as we saw it, too young. We demanded to know, as if our lives being cut short were a far greater loss than if we had lived to old age. Cut *short*, Giáp! Who's to say they were? How short is short? Would my death at nineteen be any less traumatic to my family if it had happened at twenty-nine, thirty-nine, forty-nine, or later? Wouldn't they be happy for me if they knew it wasn't the end but a new beginning? How arrogant of us to assume mortal death is tragic, losing our souls, if that's even possible. Perhaps it is, but I don't think so. Mortal death is not the end."

Giáp listened carefully to what Raymond said and could wait no longer to respond.

"If a soul can die, what remains? No, I now understand that mortal death is transformative, the end of one phase of life, the beginning of another—a 'bridge' to our immortal unlived lives. We must learn to cross this bridge, leading An, Eden, Shelly, and many others with us. I don't know exactly how we do that, but I believe it's more about the journey than the destination."

CHAPTER FIFTY-FOUR

OTHER WORLDS, ALWAYS A VAST, FLUID SPACE, TIMELESS AND unrestricted. The pulsating hum, once again anticipating Giáp, Raymond, Shelly, An, and Eden, will fill the familiar, now-empty, overstuffed leather chairs.

Unlike before, no vortex calling anyone to enter. They are beyond that now. No doors, windows, or visible light fixtures—no restrictions. Only whispers of their past lives, mingling with those of the ones they love.

Gradually, Raymond's image becomes clear, a calm, peaceful expression on his face. Soon after, Giáp joins him, the two of them together, each at ease with the other, offering hope to everyone else.

Shelly, Eden, and An appear, settling into their seats with their own questions and fears. Raymond speaks.

"Previously, when you were called here, it was to challenge and encourage you to be honest with each other and yourselves. Failing to do so meant you would find no answers to your questions. Today is different. I called Giáp to be here with me. I challenged both of us to confront our relationship and our purpose. Having done so, we discovered much in common. We identified the next step we all must take searching for our immortal futures. As always, you do not have to follow us. You can leave whenever you wish, returning to wherever you were in the multiverse before your first visit to Other Worlds. We hope you will at least listen before deciding what you want to do."

Raymond sat down, a signal to Giáp to continue their explanation to Shelly, An, and Eden.

"As Raymond said, he challenged us to be honest with each other. I will be more specific than he was with me. He was referring to us having brutally killed each other. What did that mean? Did we stop the war? We did not. I could list several things we failed to accomplish, but none would matter compared to what we did. The death of our mortal bodies was the vehicle for that transformation. We no longer exist as mortals, nor do any of you who have accepted the invitation to be here in Other Worlds. As Raymond said, it is a place you can still choose to leave whenever you wish. If you stay, you will help all of us find our immortal places in the multiverse."

Once again, standing next to Giáp, Raymond continued.

"Our mortal deaths are beginnings, part of an endless thread of life that begins at creation and continues through our mortal births, deaths, and our souls' search for their places in the multiverse. You've all experienced grief. But that is just a byproduct of growth; without it, none of us could ever find immortality. Do not attempt to ignore it; you will fail. Your grief will pass, and when it does, you will keep moving forward. Mortal death is a 'bridge' to immortality that most souls cross when it is their time. But some do not know how to cross it. Giáp will tell each of you how you can help those who don't know how to help themselves."

"My role is to mentor the importance of forgiveness and accepting the mortal death of others as part of natural transformation. Shelly, you must teach that transformation. Mortal death should be accepted and welcomed when it naturally occurs, a time not set by mortals. You have been chosen for this because you committed suicide. Now, it is your responsibility to teach others not to do the same.

"An, you will teach others that their identity does not define their purpose. You saw yourself as a child cheated of a father. You weren't cheated; that was your fate. Your purpose is to share that experience, helping others remove the burden they carry.

"Eden, having never been born, you have no collective memory for the past you never lived. But you have now created your past with Shelly and Raymond. Others can do as you have done. Help them discover memories of events they never experienced.

"Raymond, who began this journey with me, will describe his purpose to you."

"Giáp guided me through journeys exploring alternate lives I could have lived had I made different choices. This brought clarity to my mind and led me to you, Shelly. I will do the same for other souls lost in the multiverse, seeking their partner souls. There is much for all of you to consider before deciding whether to continue with us or return to your lives as you knew them. Please think carefully, asking any questions you like. This is important to you, to all of us, and to so many like us who are lost in the multiverse."

CHAPTER FIFTY-FIVE

"EDEN."

"Yes, An."

"We have reached the same conclusion, haven't we? I believe so, but I want to be sure before I act. I can't search for my eternal existence, having lived so little of my mortal life. Do you see that? I want to know what you think."

"You are the only one of us whose mortal existence is logical. I was never born. Your father was killed before you were born. But you *were* born, An. You began a mortal life. You were there for your mother when she needed you most. There is much you should still do before you search for your immortal life. The others and I are different from you. We have no choice, but you do. You have not completed your mortal journey. I haven't either, because I never lived a mortal life, not one day of it."

"I know. I just needed to hear you say it. But I can't imagine what it will be like to go back to my mortal life without you. Giáp and Raymond both say those who do will have no memory of their search for immortality. That means I will not be with you. I will not remember having been with you. I don't know which is worse, having no memory of you or leaving my mortal life too soon. If I stay, will that guarantee that our unlived lives will be together?"

"I don't know, An. Maybe Giáp or Raymond can answer that. I

don't believe there are guarantees for any of this. All they have said is that we each have things we must do that are, in different ways, unique to us. If so, what is mine cannot be yours, and what is yours cannot be mine."

"I've thought about this a lot during the time we spent in Other Worlds. I had not questioned anything that had happened to me. My father, whom I believed had died after abandoning my mother and me, suddenly reappeared. I was a young boy then, and I did not fully trust or believe what he told me. But over the years, he proved his words through his actions. He no longer existed, yet somehow he had entered my mortal consciousness, forcing me to decide what to do. What does that say about being mortal versus immortal? How did his existence and mine reconnect?"

"Does understanding matter? Isn't what he has done more important, whether or not you understand why? I don't understand my situation. I was never born, and yet here I am, having to make the same decision you do without knowing the consequences. You look for certainty where none exists."

"You are right. Either way, I have to decide what to do. Please help me. Whatever I choose will affect both of us."

"Yes, it will, but all I know for sure is that you will know when it's time to leave a place, person, or situation. Do not underestimate the importance of what you choose. Do not delay changing something you know is wrong. Doing so is a decision, the consequences of which could end your ability to choose your eternal life."

CHAPTER FIFTY-SIX

Other Worlds is a place for self-reflection before making decisions that affect not only the decision-maker but also everyone they will meet in their mortal and immortal lives. Gradually, Giáp, Raymond, Shelly, Eden, and An appear, each sensing the weight of what is to come. Giáp's eyes search An's face, finding resolve and sadness. Raymond stands quietly, shoulders squared, eyes gentle with understanding. Shelly and Eden keep their gaze steady, both feeling the impending separation from what they hold dear.

As before, all are together again in Other Worlds, anticipating something significant was about to happen. Each sat in their leather chairs, their positions hinting at what was about to occur. Four of them arranged in a semicircle, facing An.

Giáp spoke first.

"Raymond and I provided you all with the information we have to help each of you decide what to do. Continue your search for the immortal future you envisioned, helping others who are lost just as you are, or choose to return to a mortal life. If you choose the latter, you will have no memory of your time in Other Worlds. If you were unhappy in that life before, you will be again. Whether that changes depends on how you choose to live whatever time remains to you as a mortal. All of you have made your choices, and we will learn what those are for each of us, starting with An."

An stood up from his chair, his eyes gradually locking onto each of them until he reached Eden. The two of them searched one last time to see if anything had changed since their private discussion. He began to speak.

"I can't imagine anything more difficult than what I am about to say to you. But as the mortal I am, I am convinced I have made the right choice for you and for me."

Eden's and An's eyes briefly met before Eden quickly looked away to her left, away from An and the others, as he continued.

"I wonder whether being mortal—the only one of us who is—means that not searching for immortality before all of this began makes deciding what to do easier or harder. Someone whose opinion I highly value recently asked me, 'Does understanding matter?' The answer is no, it doesn't. We all know everything we can know, which isn't the same as knowing everything there is to know. The time has come for each of us to decide whether to keep searching for our immortal life or return to our mortal existence. I choose the latter, a decision based on incomplete knowledge and assumptions. Part of me wishes I believed I could make a positive difference by helping others with their search if I stayed with all of you. I don't feel I can. My mortal life is unfinished, while all of yours have ended or never began. You might wish you could revisit the lives you lived and some of your unlived lives to change the choices you made. I can't do that; my mortal past is incomplete. I must go back to finish my mortality before I can start searching for my immortality."

An paused, making one last attempt to confirm whether what he was saying and doing was right. He looked at each person individually, hoping someone would reassure him that he had made the right choice. His eyes rested on Giáp, his father, and he heard his voice speak words to his heart the others could not hear.

You will know when it is time to leave a place, person, or situation. Do not put off changing something you know is wrong. Doing so is a decision, the consequences of which will end your ability to choose your immortal life. You have made your choice known, An. If you are comfortable with it, it is the right choice. Our souls live in both our mortal and immortal selves. I will always know you; you will always know me. We will not lose that connection.

We may one day reunite when your mortal life ends, whether you are moving into your immortal life or continuing your search for eternal life. However, it is now time for you to state your choice clearly.

"I will return to my mortal life believing that when that is naturally over, a time I will not choose, we will all be reunited somewhere in the vast, infinite multiverse."

He sat in his chair, unsure of what would come next, as he watched the others fade away. Silence filled Other Worlds until the unmistakable hum grew louder inside the globe, flowing all around him. He stood, turning away from where the others had sat, all now gone. He was alone, facing the small pinpoint of light that grew larger by the moment, moving closer, beckoning him to step into it, engulfing him. His time in Other Worlds, in the multiverse, was not finished, but it was over for now.

Giáp, Raymond, Shelly, and Eden stood silently, gazing at the fading light where An had been moments earlier. Their expressions showed sorrow and respect, knowing An's decision was final—the right choice for him. A shared sense of closure filled them—their individual paths continued, but in this moment they honored An's courage in accepting his mortal fate, trusting that his choice aligned with the larger eternal truth they all sought.

"Your work is beautiful. You have great talent!"

Eden looked up and saw an Asian man, whom she guessed was about her age, looking over her shoulder at the building she was drawing. She hadn't heard him approach; he seemed to appear out of nowhere.

"Thank you. I hope everyone who views my art feels the same way you do. However, judging by how many buy, that might not be the case."

“Well, unfortunately, I cannot afford to buy, but I appreciate what you are doing. My name is An.”

"Good to meet you, An. I'm Eden."

"You have no accent. Where are you from?"

"No," Eden sighed, "I'm a little bit from everywhere, too much to be from anywhere. What about you?

An laughed, "I like that, can I *not* be from anywhere as well?"

"Of course, why not?"

Eden found An interesting. She wanted to ask where in Asia he was from, but decided not to, thinking it might be intrusive.

"You see what I do for a living; what do you do?"

“What I do or how I make money to live? They are not the same.”

"You answer my questions with questions. Are you a mystic?"

An smiled before answering, "Yes, we all are in different and wonderful ways. Are you here every day? I would like to continue talking with you. Maybe one day soon I will have enough money to honor your talent properly by buying something from you."

"I’m somewhere around here most days, except Wednesdays. You don't have to buy anything. I've enjoyed your company and the break from drawing. Enjoy the rest of your day, An. I hope to see you soon."

"You as well, Eden, and you will see me again, soon."

This was the last and only time Eden and An would see each other.

CHAPTER FIFTY-SEVEN

For the first time in years, Raymond found new purpose in his life, happy to have moved to New York City, where he lived in a walk-up on the Lower East Side, less than half the size of his Seattle apartment.

Well, I'm more of a have-not than a have, so this is what I must accept. I'm okay with it; most of my life will be spent in the city, anyway, not just looking at it from my apartment window.

More than just a change of address, Raymond decided to pursue a new career as an adjunct counselor with the NYC Department of Veterans' Affairs. He had been helped getting the job by someone doing similar work in Seattle—a man with contacts at the Veterans' Affairs office in NYC. Raymond often wondered what his life would have been like had he moved to New York after being in the service. But, as usual, he postponed making the decision to move, continuing to live unhappily in Seattle without knowing why or what to do about it. No longer.

I don't know how this will turn out, but at least I won't have to look back and wonder 'what if?' I'm here now and will make the best of it.

His first week in Manhattan was overwhelming. So many people moving so quickly, far more than in Seattle. But this pushed him to become one of them, not apart from them.

"Welcome, Raymond, or do you prefer to be called Ray?" Arlin Gettle, the psychologist who would mentor and oversee Raymond, said as he walked into his office and found Raymond waiting for him. Raymond stood to greet him, and the two men shook hands.

"Either works, and I'm rarely consistent about what I go by. I answer to both."

"Good to hear. I believe they told you we'll be working together, but just in case, I'm Arlin Gettle, a staff psychologist, a very overworked one. That's why I requested someone with your background be assigned to help me."

"I received this general position description, which includes your name and title," Raymond said, handing the paper to Arlin.

After a brief look, Arlin replied.

"Good, I wrote that. I hope it gave you enough to have a reasonable, if not complete, expectation of what you'll be doing," he said, sitting down behind his desk, the two of them now facing each other. Raymond sat down as well.

"It did. I knew there would be more detail, but this was a good start."

"Great. What it doesn't tell you is what you *won't* be doing. Let me give you a quick overview to start. I chose you because you served in the army, in combat in Vietnam with the 101st Airborne. I understand that was a challenging time for you. I wouldn't have wished that on you, but because you've had that experience, you should be able to relate well to those who have and are now having difficulty adjusting to civilian life. My role is to identify the specific psychological difficulty they are experiencing, provide counsel, and help them cope. I'm trained for that; you are not. Your role is to listen to them and share your experiences. Often, just talking with someone who has gone through similar circumstances and emerged well-adjusted helps with their own recovery. You are somewhere between a counselor and a friend, with more emphasis on the latter and less on the former. Does all this make sense so far?"

"It does, and that is what I expected when I interviewed for the position. I know there is much more to learn, but this is a good start."

"Yes, there's quite a bit more, including a three-week orientation, followed by you shadowing me as I meet with clients. Again, you don't do that to do what I do; you'd need to go back to school for that. It's more about listening to what they say, observing how they respond to what I tell them. You'll do that for another two to three weeks, and if all goes as I hope and expect, you'll go solo after that. Any questions?"

"Yes, a lot, actually," Ray said, smiling. "But I'm sure most of them will be answered during orientation or while working with you. I'm looking forward to starting."

"Aside from the work part, I understand you're new to our wonderful city, right? Any questions about it that I, a true native New Yorker, can help you with?"

Ray smiled. "Be careful what you offer, Arlin. I have more questions about the city than about this job. But for now, no. I've settled into an apartment on the Lower East Side. I've spent some time in Manhattan over the years and know my way around. But I'll definitely take you up on your offer for restaurants and a few other things."

"I can handle that when the time comes. Come with me to meet the guy who leads the orientation. He'll brief you on that, including your start date. Until then, I have a few things I'd like you to read here in the office, and at home once orientation begins."

CHAPTER FIFTY-EIGHT

TWO WEEKS INTO HIS NEW JOB AND ONE WEEK INTO HIS THREE-WEEK orientation, Raymond was learning more about his duties and exploring the area around his apartment. Most of his past visits to Manhattan had him staying in Midtown on the West Side. The Lower East Side was less familiar to him, but he could see it had a more neighborhood-like vibe than Midtown, with more residential neighborhoods, parks, grocery stores, and restaurants. In previous years, after work, all of Lower Manhattan would clear out, with the people who worked there leaving for the night. Now, they have the option to live near their workplaces, as Raymond was doing.

Living in NYC, he vowed not to trap himself in his apartment as he had in Seattle.

I may be in early middle age, but as the song says, If I can make it here, I can make it anywhere. There's a social life out there waiting for me; I will find it.

He chose an apartment just off Gold Street near Maiden Lane for its proximity to work, subways, and FDR Drive. This allowed him to take advantage of what he knew he should have done while living in Seattle: walking along the waterfront early in the morning and in the evenings before and after work. It gave him time to mentally prepare for the day ahead and unwind afterward.

This is beautiful—the Brooklyn Bridge in front of me, the East River to my right, and Brooklyn just beyond. I experienced something similar in Seattle, even closer, but I rarely took advantage of it. I will here.

Time passed quickly for Raymond since his move to New York. He completed his three-week orientation, and after two weeks of observing Arlin work with clients, they agreed it was time for him to work independently.

The task was, as Arlin said it would be on the first day in his office: listen to what the client has to say, and, when appropriate, share his own experiences. Raymond was busy doing that every day. The workload exceeded available resources, something Arlin said he would soon discover. He also told Raymond that it was vital not to let his relationship with clients extend outside the office.

"Stay strictly professional, Raymond. No calling or hanging out. If they suggest otherwise, tell them that VAO rules prohibit contact outside the office. If they persist, let me know, and I'll handle it."

Raymond understood why this was important. Letting a relationship extend beyond contact in the VAO office could undermine his purpose. He was meant to serve as a sounding board for things clients might not share with Arlin. He wasn't there to judge, only to listen, and when appropriate, to offer examples from his past for the client to follow.

Raymond arrived at the office forty-five minutes before his first appointment, the last day of his fourth week working alone. He was happy with how things were going, knowing Arlin was, too. Raymond didn't expect anything unusual this morning. He would be meeting Jordan Kale, age 63, a veteran himself and the father of Brayden Kale, who had died in Iraq five years earlier.

To this point, all the clients Raymond had worked with were younger than Jordan. Their issues centered on their own experiences. Jordan served twelve years in the Army before retiring nearly thirty years ago. He deployed overseas once but did not personally see combat. His son told his parents he joined the Army because his dad did. He was killed in Iraq when the vehicle he was in hit an Improvised Explosive Device (IED) placed in the road just outside the International Zone, called "the green zone"—a ten-square-kilometer, heavily fortified area in the Karkh district of central Baghdad.

CHAPTER FIFTY-NINE

RAYMOND PICKED UP THE PHONE ON ITS FIRST RING.

"Good morning, Carol. What do you have for me?"

"Good morning to you, Raymond. Just letting you know, Mr. Kale, your first appointment this morning is here."

"Great, on time, early actually; we're off to a good start. Send him in."

Carol opened the door, and Jordan Kale entered. Raymond moved around his desk to greet him.

"Good morning, Jordan. I hope you don't mind my calling you that. Let me know if you do. My name is Raymond Quinn."

"Happy to meet you, Raymond, and I prefer you use my first name."

They shook hands, and Raymond sat in his chair, gesturing for Jordan to take a seat in front of his desk.

"First of all, thank you for arriving early; many don't, and as the day goes on, we tend to fall behind."

"Not a problem. I am compulsively early. I can't stand being late."

"We have that in common. I know you've had a few visits with Arlin, and I hope things are going well for both of you. He shared a background summary about you, including why you're here. I've read it, but I'd like to hear more from you directly to ensure we're all on the same page."

"I have met with Arlin four times now. I enjoy working with him, and from what he tells me, I will working with you as well."

"That's good to hear. I imagine he told you the difference between what he does and what I do."

"He did. I believe I understand."

"Just to confirm, I'll review everything once more. If you notice anything different from what Arlin said, let me know. We want to clarify that early to prevent misunderstandings. Arlin is a psychologist; I am not. The two of you will discuss issues with him from a clinical standpoint. He doesn't share details with me about that, except to update me on your progress. You and I will have a 'civilian' conversation about why you are here. By civilian, I mean I am not trained as Arlin is. However, I have experienced similar situations to yours, so discussing some of that might be helpful. Arlin and I will review your progress to see if our observations align. If they don't, we'll look further into it to ensure you feel you are receiving the help you need and expect. How does that sound compared to what you and Arlin discussed?"

"Very close. I like the process and appreciate you taking the time to explain the goal."

"Before we continue, do you have any questions you'd like to ask me?"

"I hadn't thought about it, but since you mention it, Arlin said you were in the service. He thought some of your experience might apply to my situation."

"I was in the army before you. I believe their advertising called it 'The New Action Army,' something like that. I'm not sure how 'new' it really was, or how much 'action' there was compared with when my father served in World War II. For me, it was just a lot of 'hurry up and wait,'" Raymond said, a look of disappointment on his face.

Jordan burst out laughing.

"That is so true, no matter when you serve. My time was 'Be all you can be.' Once, during basic training, I had to be in the mess hall at three a.m. for KP. The mess sergeant told me to wet-mop the entire mess hall floor, including moving all the chairs from under the tables and putting them back when I was done, all within an hour. There were about forty tables, and I don't remember how many chairs, but definitely too many to finish in an hour. Trying to be funny, I said, 'Sarge, is this really all I can be?' He didn't laugh, and the tension between us only grew from there."

Raymond smiled, nodding in agreement.

"Oh, I know. I never met a mess sergeant with a sense of humor. But I don't suppose I would have either, getting up so early, staying so late, feeding a hundred or more idiots who didn't appreciate my food. Is there anything else you'd like to ask before we get started? I will likely tell you more about my time in the army as we go along, but feel free to ask whatever else you might want to know now."

"No, thank you, Raymond, time to get to work."

"Call me, Ray. I've reviewed Arlin's summary of your background, including your son's. Would you mind going over that again in light of why you're here?"

"Not at all. Let me know if I'm sharing more than you want or need. You know I was in the army for twelve years. When Brayden was eighteen, he told his mother and me he wanted to join the army, serve three years, then get out and attend college, using the GI Bill to help pay for it. He added, 'I also want to serve because you did, Dad.'"

He paused, looking down, trying to gather his emotions before continuing.

"I was pleased he acknowledged my service as one reason for wanting to enlist. I also saw value in his plan to use the GI Bill to cover some of his college expenses. My wife, his mother, was not at all happy about any of it. She told Brayden she did not want him to join any branch of the military. She was adamant; there was no room for discussion. The three of us talked about it occasionally, with no change in our positions. Brayden and I agreed; his mother did not. Soon after a particularly long, heated discussion, Brayden brought the subject up again at dinner with a major twist. He had signed his army enlistment papers that day and would report in two weeks."

"I'm sure that went over well with Mom," Raymond replied, a hint of sarcasm in his voice.

"Oh, you have no idea. She was furious with him and with me for, in her view, secretly encouraging him to enlist without telling her beforehand. I didn't say anything to Brayden that she didn't hear herself. He told her I didn't, that he had gone ahead with it on his own. He said he was eighteen, tired of all the arguments, none of which changed his mind, and he enlisted."

Although much of what Jordan said was in Arlin's report, Raymond initially thought the conflict was more about an unresolved dispute between him and his wife, which the report did not address. Jordan looked down, his head bowed, clearly struggling not to cry. Raymond opened his desk drawer, took out a box of tissues, and set it directly in front of Jordan on the desk.

"Jordan, I know from Arlin's report that there's more to the story. It will bring out emotions you can't hold back. Please don't try to disguise them. Cry, scream, whatever you feel like doing. Chances are, I've done some or all of that myself. The tissues are there if you need them."

Jordan slowly looked up at the tissue box, taking one of them to wipe tears from his cheeks.

"Thank you, Ray. I don't mean to cry; I do all I can to keep from crying. It just happens. Not because of what I've told you so far, but because of the rest of the story."

"Whatever makes you comfortable, Jordan, that's why I'm here. Let me give you an option. We have about twenty more minutes today. You can continue if you wish or wait until our next session; the choice is yours. If we continue, we will need to stop at ten because I have another client waiting for me."

"I understand. Let's wait until next time to continue; there's more I want you to know. The problem isn't with my wife and me; it's me alone."

"Certainly. If you'd like, I can use the remaining time to expand a bit on my service."

Jordan sat upright, composed, with a slight smile beginning to show, making Raymond think of the sun breaking through rain clouds after a storm.

"Yes, I'd like to hear that, including any mess hall stories you might have."

"No mess hall stories, but after we get to know each other better and if you promise not to tell anyone else, I do have a few things I could share with you, some of which might explain why I didn't get promoted as often as some of the others."

Jordan laughed again, the earlier tension now gone.

"I was drafted and served in the infantry with the 101st Airborne Division in Vietnam. And before you ask, no, I was not airborne-qualified. Except for a few long-range patrol and ranger units, the 101st was taken off airborne status while in Vietnam. Like the 1st Cavalry Division, the 101st was an airmobile division. Wherever we went, we traveled by helicopter."

"Either way, that must have been something."

"Yes, and no; as I said earlier, it was a lot of hurry-up-and-wait. Others have said this before, and it's true. Ninety-five percent of my time in Vietnam was incredibly boring, with the remaining five percent off-the-chart terrifying. But I survived it."

Raymond looked at his watch.

"That's all the time we have today, Jordan, but I think we're off to a good start. I hope you do, too."

"I do, Ray. I'm glad I'll be working with Arlin and you. I look forward to our next session."

"Me too, Jordan. Good to meet you. Stop by Carol's desk; she'll set us up to meet again. I'm looking forward to it."

CHAPTER SIXTY

After work, Raymond walked along the East River on FDR Drive, enjoying a comfortably warm early-spring evening. It was a way to clear his mind before dinner at one of the many Italian restaurants he frequented near his apartment.

His time with VAO clients was generally as he expected. However, his encounter with Jordan was different in some ways. The others had sad stories to share, and after reading Arlin's summary, Raymond knew Jordan's would probably be as well, likely in their next meeting. But there was something about Jordan that Raymond did not feel about the others.

Maybe it was because he was today's first appointment? I don't know why that would matter. Certainly, his son's death, but there's something more.

He continued thinking about Jordan while having dinner at Bene Sicily, an Italian restaurant he liked, a short walk from home. Not in a hurry to return to his apartment, he ordered a second glass of Chianti after the waiter cleared his dishes.

I'll pay closer attention to him when we meet again. I might be overlooking something important.

Raymond checked his schedule for the next day and reviewed his and Arlin's notes from previous client visits. This helped him guide his questions rather than just reacting to what the client said. He needed to ensure he questioned anything that seemed out of place based on their previous visits. He saw that Jordan was on tomorrow's schedule, as before, the first appointment. Looking at Arlin's notes, he saw the following:

Three times, Jordan referred to his son, Brayden, as if he were still alive. After the second time, I pointed it out, and he smiled, saying it was just a mistake; he knew he had died. I didn't mention it the third time, but I will if it happens again.

Raymond thought this was important enough to call Arlin at home to discuss before meeting with Jordan the next day.

"I'm sorry to bother you at home, Arlin, but I have a meeting with Jordan first thing tomorrow morning. After reading your notes, especially where you mention he referred to Brayden three times as if Brayden were still alive, I wanted to ask for your opinion on how I should respond if he does the same with me. Specifically, is it okay for me to point it out to him, as you did, and watch for his reaction?"

"No bother, Ray. We won't have time to discuss it before you see him tomorrow, so now's a good time. I don't think mentioning it will be a problem; in fact, I'm curious to see how he reacts to you versus me. Don't push it; pay attention to what he says, his facial expressions, and body language, all typical cues. He does get emotional—watch for that as well."

"Yes, he does. I'll watch closely to see whether it differs from what I've seen before. Has he said anything else about his wife?"

"I know there are issues between them, but what do you mean specifically?"

"He said his wife was furious with him, accusing him of having separate conversations with Brayden, encouraging him to enlist without discussing it with her first. Has he said anything about that to you?"

"Nothing to do with her being furious, but he made it clear that she blames him for Brayden enlisting and, by extension, his death. I'm glad you mentioned it. I need to talk to him about that when we meet the end of next week. Thank you. And please take note of everything he says and does—facial expressions, body language, and any subtle shifting in his chair; it helps to be aware of all of that."

"I will. I don't have enough experience to say this definitively, but after three weeks of client meetings—about sixty in total—something feels different about my time with Jordan compared with the others. That, more than anything, is why I'm glad you had time to talk about it tonight."

"Again, not a problem, Ray. I'm glad you called. It shows you're not just in it for the paycheck. Anything else? I've got the time if you do."

"No, that covers it. I'll pay close attention during my session with him tomorrow and summarize it in my notes. We can discuss it afterward if you'd like. Have a good night."

"You too, Ray."

CHAPTER SIXTY-ONE

"GOOD MORNING, JORDAN. HOW'S YOUR WEEK BEEN?"

"Not bad, actually pretty good. How about you?"

"Couldn't be better. I relocated here for this job from Seattle. I lived downtown there, too. Seattle is a mid-sized 'big' city, but it's nothing compared to Manhattan. This wasn't a shock to me; I've been here several times. I'm adjusting well. I could have looked it up in your file. If you don't mind me asking, where do you live, and where are you from if not here?"

"Born and raised in New Orleans, transplanted to Brooklyn when my parents moved there in the late 'fifties. It was a cultural shock for them at the time. I graduated from LSU, more my parents' choice than my own, followed by twelve years in the army."

"Interesting, and I don't mean that just to be conversational. Do you know what caused your parents to move to such a different place compared with New Orleans?"

"A job; my dad taught economics at Brooklyn College."

"I've been to New Orleans and driven through Louisiana. The transition from there to metro NYC must have been a big shock for your parents. Did your mother work outside the home?"

"Yes, and no. She was, and still is, a freelance writer working from home. Perfect for her. No need to commute like my dad did. Not far, but far enough for him to complain about it."

"Which is why I decided I would live no farther from my job than I could walk most days. Good exercise. I can do it most any day, except when it rains or snows too much. Shall we get to the official part of our time together?"

"Absolutely."

"You were telling me about Brayden finally deciding to enlist, tired of the discussion and arguing among the three of you. You said there was something that made it hard for you to control your emotions. You also said there was more to it; I believe you called it 'the rest of the story.' Have you and Arlin talked about that? I don't see it referenced in his notes."

Jordan looked down at the floor before replying.

"Not really. I'll be honest. I don't like talking about it because it often makes me break down."

"It sounds as though 'it,' whatever it is, is important. Uncomfortable for you, but important for Arlin to know to help you. Do you agree?"

Jordan sat, tapping the fingers of his left hand as though playing a piano, showing no emotion. Raymond said nothing more for a minute or so before responding.

"I'm sure you know this, Jordan, but the things that make you most uncomfortable are exactly what you and Arlin need to discuss. At least enough to rule them out as possible reasons you are here. You and I can avoid some of those topics, but you shouldn't with Arlin. I don't want you to think that he or I are betraying you by sharing what you've said between us. However, even if you feel it is a betrayal, we do it to help you. Do you understand?"

Jordan stopped tapping his fingers and looked up at Raymond. He couldn't tell whether the expression on Jordan's face was relief or anger. Before speaking, he sighed and looked up at the ceiling.

"God, I knew this would happen. When it didn't immediately with Arlin, I felt relieved. I thought the thing I most wanted to avoid discussing wasn't related to my problem. At least I hoped it wasn't. Maybe that's true. Maybe not," he looked back at Raymond. "What's funny, Ray, is, you don't know what 'it' is, and yet you know that's why I'm here. And you'll tell Arlin that it is." He looked down again to avoid meeting Raymond's gaze, his voice quieter. "There's no avoiding it, is there?"

Raymond allowed both of them time to process what Jordan said before replying.

"There is with me, Jordan, Arlin as well. Neither of us will force you to talk about anything you'd rather avoid. But it is his job, and by extension mine as well, to make sure you understand what we believe might be the root of your problem."

Ray stood up, turned his back to Jordan, and looked out the window.

"How's this for a bad analogy? When you have a toothache, you must choose between doing nothing or visiting a dentist to figure out the best course of action. What the dentist says you must do might include you experiencing some pain worse than what you felt before. But once the treatment is done, all pain will be gone." He turned back, facing Jordan, and continued. "Ok, back to you. You don't have dental problems, and Arlin and I are not dentists. What do you want to do?"

"I understand what you're saying. I'm fairly certain about what I want to do. Can we take a five-minute break so I can think it over and be sure?"

"Absolutely. I want coffee. Can I bring you one?"

"Yes, thank you."

"How do you take it?"

"Black is good."

"Got it. I'll be back in a few minutes. When I return, let me know if you need more time. You don't have to decide today what you want to do." Raymond said, leaving the room and closing the door behind him.

Raymond intentionally left Jordan alone for longer than the five minutes he requested. He believed that whatever Jordan was thinking about led him to seek help. He also knew he needed to be careful about what he said when they reunited.

Their coffees in both hands, Raymond lightly kicked the door, hoping Jordan would know to open it. He did, and Raymond handed him his coffee before moving behind his desk, both of them sitting down.

"I have this theory that no office coffee is ever good, especially in offices like this one that rely on outside funding. But I have to say, I've found VAO coffee to be pretty good."

Jordan took a sip. "Not bad at all," quickly bringing the discussion back to why he was there.

"I'm sure you want to know what I'm thinking. I either need to tell you everything about my situation or just not come anymore." He took a deep breath and looked directly at Raymond. "I don't know what to do, Ray."

Raymond took a sip of his coffee, hoping that not responding immediately would ease whatever Jordan was feeling. He set his coffee cup on his desk and replied.

"I'm not surprised. Whatever this is weighs heavily on you. You're right to hold off making your decision until you feel more certain about what to do."

Raymond saw the relief on Jordan's face.

"I have a suggestion, Jordan—something that has worked for me in similar situations. I dislike going to bed, trying to sleep while worrying about a problem I'm facing. However, I've found that sometimes this is exactly what I should do—hoping to push it into my subconscious by dreaming about it. Go to bed when you're so tired you think you'll fall asleep immediately. Just before you do, focus on this issue. Hopefully, answers you don't have now will come to you in your dreams. The worst that can happen is you might lose a little sleep. What do you think?"

"I have nothing to lose. I'm not sleeping well anyway. Sure, I'll try it."

"Good. You know the drill: see Carol for your next appointment. I look forward to hearing if this helps you."

CHAPTER SIXTY-TWO

Jordan did as Raymond suggested. His long day began with their meeting in Raymond's office, then to his own to tackle the growing backlog on his desk. He skipped lunch, worked late, had a quick dinner alone at home, and went to bed just after eleven p.m.

Okay, I'm tired. It won't be hard to lie here thinking about my problem. The question is, will I dream about it?

You will, Jordan, let yourself sleep now.

What is this place?

Other Worlds Coffee.

I was supposed to come here, wasn't I?

Only if you chose to, no one forced you to come.

There's no furniture, no people, no windows or doors. Everything is so white, the walls and floor blending into each other.

Turn around, Jordan, face, and walk toward the light. It will take you where you must go.

The light, a pinhole growing larger, brighter, coming towards me.

Walk into the light, Jordan.

This was not your fault, Dad. I chose this, not you.

It cost you your life, Brayden. Your mother blames me. We both feel terrible and miss you so much.

My mortal life, Dad, but that is not the end of my being. I exist in the multiverse. You and Mother do, too, in one universe, living your mortal lives as I once did. I have to continue my search. You will both pass from mortal to immortal life in your own time, as I have. When you do, we will be together again. But it must be your own time, a time you cannot alter. If you do, your search will not lead you to my soul. Let it be, Dad.

CHAPTER SIXTY-THREE

THE WEEK SINCE JORDAN'S LAST APPOINTMENT WITH RAYMOND PASSED quickly, and both were eager to meet again this morning. Raymond hoped to hear that Jordan had made up his mind about what to discuss with him and Arlin. Jordan looked forward to sharing his decision with Raymond.

"How about we start this morning by getting more of that coffee we had last week?"

"I was going to request that; put it on my tab, Ray."

Back in Raymond's office, the small talk about each of their past week was now over, and Jordan could wait no longer.

"Ray, you told me to try to dream about my problem. After our meeting, I went to my office, more tired than I realized. I stayed to catch up on work until after nine-thirty. It was past ten when I got home. I had a quick leftover dinner alone and went to bed, feeling very tired. I suppose I fell asleep quickly. I don't recall lying awake or dreaming. But I definitely did dream. The next morning, I woke up feeling more refreshed than I had in a long time."

"Great news, Jordan. You say you had a dream. Do you remember what it was about?"

"I do, and that's the wonderful part. I dreamed I spoke with Brayden. I told him his mother and I are still grieving, missing him so much. He said he is fine existing in the multiverse. His mortal life is over; he is searching for his immortal life. He said the three of us will reunite when our mortal lives naturally end. I don't understand all of this, but I do enough to feel much better. I explained this to my wife, telling her that you had advised me to dream about what troubles me so I could find a solution. I said I did and that I had spoken with Brayden. She initially rejected everything I said, but soon after, she accepted it because thinking about it made her feel better. Thank you, Ray. You made all this possible."

"I'm glad to hear that, Jordan, but it wasn't me. You and your wife achieved this with Brayden's help. You never considered that your wife could help you find a solution or that Brayden might be able to help both of you. Death does not eliminate that possibility. It only happened when you finally opened yourself to new thinking. Never forget this, Jordan. It will help you the next time you are in crisis."

CHAPTER SIXTY-FOUR

"I LIKED IT BETTER WHEN ONE OF THOSE LARGE, OVERSTUFFED LEATHER chairs you had to be very lucky to find unoccupied, suddenly appeared after I picked up my coffee," Kathy said to the younger woman standing next to her in line to order.

"That sounds much better than standing. I haven't seen them at any of the Starbucks I've visited recently. It must have been before I moved here. You're right. Hot coffee would be much more enjoyable while sitting down."

"They started removing them over three years ago. It's very expensive to keep them clean of spilled drinks and food, and probably worse. All that, plus the cost of replacing them. I'm Kathy, and it's nice to have someone to talk to even while standing."

"Nice to meet you, Kathy. I'm Shelly."

"Do you live here, or are you visiting? By the way, I love your accent."

"Thank you. The rest of my life? I don't know for certain. I've lived here most of the past year. I'm from Zimbabwe in southern Africa."

"Really, how interesting. What made you decide to move to Seattle?"

"I'm not sure. For reasons I can't explain, just a long-standing belief, this is where I should be. I tried other places, including a few where I thought I would stay with people I imagined myself being with forever. But in each of those situations, I couldn't shake the feeling that I should be here. So, why fight it? Here I am," she said, smiling. "I assume you do, too. Do you live here in downtown or the suburbs?"

"Rainier Beach, south of downtown, in a small house near Lake Washington. Do you know the area?"

"I don't. I rented an apartment south of Lake Union. I don't know where I'd like to be, but I won't be there for long. For now, it's just a place to store my few belongings and to sleep. I need to focus on completing the government-required tasks that would allow me to stay longer than my temporary visa does. Hopefully, permanently."

"You mean applying for citizenship? What do you need to do for that?"

"It's complicated, but the best option is to secure a job at a US company that hasn't been able to find a qualified US citizen applicant. I have a chance with Boeing, though I wouldn't if I weren't African. My degree is in process applications, and many applicants have similar credentials. I've had two interviews, and it helps that I'm from Africa. The hiring manager said they could use my skills to help expand their business throughout the continent. If they hire me, they will assist with my green card application, which would enable me to stay indefinitely. If that happens, I could then apply to become a naturalized citizen."

"Very interesting. I imagine few US citizens realize how fortunate we are not to have to qualify with the government to get a job. I wish you well. I'm a little hungry. How about joining me for lunch nearby? There are plenty of options."

"I am hungry, thanks for the suggestion. There's no point in both of us eating alone. What were you planning to have?"

"Many options, but there's a small, reasonably priced Chinese restaurant in Pike Place Market. Very good if you like Chinese."

"Oh, I do. Let's go there."

Shelly and Kathy left Starbucks and were soon seated at Pike Place Chinese Cuisine, looking at menus.

"This all looks and smells so good, Kathy. Thanks for the suggestion and for including me. What do you recommend?"

"You're welcome, and thanks for keeping me company. I don't have any favorites. I usually order something with shrimp, chicken, and vegetables, but I always end up ordering too much. I take the leftovers home for later. What about you?"

"That sounds good. Please order for both of us. I'm not a big eater, and you can take home whatever we don't eat here."

Shelly and Kathy took their time eating, and with no one waiting for one of the few tables, they lingered after drinking tea.

"Kathy, this has been so enjoyable. I'm glad I met you. Can I give you my phone number so we can do something like this again?"

"Yes, certainly. I enjoyed it too, and meeting you. Here's my number; let's not wait too long to meet again. I don't know how familiar you are with downtown and the surrounding areas. I was born and raised here, so you have a built-in tour guide whenever you want."

"I've explored quite a bit, but you probably have much more to show me that I haven't considered. Even if that weren't the case, it's the company that makes the journey worthwhile."

CHAPTER SIXTY-FIVE

Boeing asked Shelly to meet with additional people she would work with and for if they offered her a position. In total, six separate meetings with eleven individuals. She had nearly given up hope of receiving an offer when she received an email from Boeing's human resources department.

16 October 2012

Ms. Shelly Bennett

I am pleased to inform you that the hiring manager has asked me to invite you back to my office for a final meeting to discuss Boeing's employment offer.

Part of the reason this process took so long is that more than one of the people you met with felt you might be a better fit for an expanded position—one with greater responsibilities. I would like to discuss that position with you in person. If, after learning the requirements, you are interested, I will also share details on compensation and other related benefits, including assistance in obtaining permanent resident status as a step toward applying for US citizenship. As you will hear when we meet, Boeing hopes to see this happen as soon as possible, given our plans for the position.

I look forward to hearing from you soon. You can contact me at my office number to arrange a convenient date and time for a meeting.

Regards,

Lenore Baker

Senior Human Resources Manager

Shelly couldn't wait to tell Kathy the news. They had become very close friends. Kathy knew Shelly was frustrated by the endless meetings and delays. She was losing hope that Boeing would ever offer her a position that would help her obtain permanent resident status. If not, her tourist visa would soon expire, forcing her to leave the US. Kathy did not want to lose her close friend.

"What are you doing for dinner tonight?" Shelly asked when Kathy answered the phone, doing her best to hide her excitement.

"Dinner? I haven't even had lunch, much less thought about dinner. I suppose leftovers from the night before last. Delicious, huh? Why? If you have a better option, which could be almost anything, please let me know."

"I believe I do. I received an email today from Boeing's Senior Human Resources Manager. The reason my interview process took so long is that the original position has been expanded to include more responsibilities and higher pay. I knew they were interested in me because I'm African, and that is a factor. Let's go out to dinner tonight, but not to celebrate. I want to wait until I know what the position is and have accepted their offer. Call this a mini celebration, to be followed by a big one once I know the outcome."

"Oh, Shelly, that's wonderful news for both of us. I hope everything works out for you. I've worried that your tourist visa will expire, and you'll be forced to leave the country. I want to hear all about it. Tell me more."

"I'm excited now, but I was worried they might not offer me anything. I have nowhere else to turn, so the timing is perfect. Let's save the rest of the story for dinner. How about that place we went to a few weeks ago, Collier's? Just off the lake, not too expensive, ideal for a small celebration. We'll go somewhere nicer once I accept their offer."

"Certainly better than my leftover leftovers. How will you get there?"

"I'll take the bus and walk to your house. Can you drive us to the restaurant?"

"I can pick you up, Shelly. No need for the bus."

"Nonsense, Kathy. That's way out of your way. No arguments. I'll take the bus and be at your house by five-thirty."

"Fine, on one condition."

"What's that?"

"I will drive you home after dinner; you're not taking the bus home. As you said, no arguments."

"Ok, win-win for both of us, see you around five-thirty."

CHAPTER SIXTY-SIX

"I'll join you at the table. I'm going to the restroom," Kathy said as they waited for the hostess to check on their table.

Looking around, Shelly thought how much she liked Collier's.

I don't know what it is, but there's something very special about this place, as if I've been here more than just a couple of times with Kathy. Is déjà vu even possible for a building?

The hostess returned, picked up two menus, and gestured for Shelly to follow her to their table. Once seated and gazing out the window, she again reflected on how she had a connection to the restaurant that went far beyond the food, the lake view, or the building—something more personal.

Kathy returned and sat down opposite Shelly, still looking out at the lake.

"You look serene. What are you thinking?"

Shelly turned to face Kathy, her expression unchanged.

"Wondering how many times you've been here?"

"Oh my gosh, I can't even imagine. But I do recall the first time. With my parents shortly after we'd moved here. I was adjusting to a new high school, hoping to make friends." She looked around the room before continuing. "But it didn't look anything like it does now. Completely redecorated. Maybe twice over the thirty years or so since that first time. If my parents and I had come only once a year, and I had continued to come once a year after they passed, that would be about sixty times. But I know I've been here more often than that. I would guess seventy-plus, now including three with you. Why do you ask?"

"I don't know. There's just something about this place that draws me in and comforts me," she said, grinning at Kathy. "Like flannel pajamas under a terry cloth robe with warm, fuzzy slippers on a cold winter night."

"That does sound good. I've got the pajamas and slippers. I'll need to get that robe; winter will be here soon."

Smiling a moment before, her expression now serious, she continued.

"I've had thoughts similar to yours about this place. A cautious, comforting feeling. I think it must be tied to having first been here with my parents and several times since, over the years. You and I have only been here together three times. I've enjoyed it, and now that you mention it, what I feel might be tied to you. How strange would that be? We've grown close in a short amount of time. I feel like I've known you forever, not just a couple of months. I even dreamed of coming here with you. We argued about something involving you and suicide. I was a little worried about you and a little angry. But we worked it out over dinner."

Hearing this sent a chill down Shelly's back.

"Kathy, you've never told me that before, have you?"

"I don't believe so. I hadn't thought about it recently, and I don't think I would have if you hadn't brought it up. I don't know when that dream happened, but it wasn't in the last month or so." She paused, a puzzled look on her face. "It feels as though it may have even occurred before we met."

Shelly forced a small, nervous laugh. "Dreaming about us being here before we even met. Spooky!" But she didn't find it funny at all.

"Kathy, is our meeting and how we're becoming such good friends so quickly just pure coincidence? Is it only me who feels there's more to it than happenstance? Why did I suggest Collier's tonight instead of one of the other nearby places we've been to? I wasn't thinking how comfortable I feel here until I was waiting for the hostess to seat me while you were in the restroom. Looking around, I relaxed completely, all tension gone. It could be about my job offer, but I wasn't thinking about that either. Whatever it was had a more déjà vu feel to it, but how can that be for a place I've only been a few times in the last few months?"

"I don't know; the world can be a very strange place at times. Speaking of your job offer, that's why we're here tonight, isn't it? Tell me about it."

Kathy was interested in Shelly's news, but she couldn't ignore the questions she had about their relationship. She felt there was something more to their connection, not just recently. It wasn't a new feeling; she had experienced something similar at Pike Place Market and in some of the restaurants she often visited. She thought it might have come from spending time downtown with her parents when she was younger.

The conversation turned to Shelly's offer letter, which she let Kathy read.

"That does sound good, and now I'm just as eager to hear what they say as you are, and a little worried. Shelly, is there a chance they'll want you to work in Africa at one of their offices? Being selfish, I'd hate to see that happen."

"Possible, yes; likely, no. I made it clear I want to migrate to the US and become a citizen. It's more likely that whatever they have in mind will involve me traveling to Africa, possibly related to customer relationships or business development. I'm okay with that as long as I can continue the citizenship process and spend most of my time in the US. I'll know more the day after tomorrow; my appointment with HR is at ten that morning."

While the evening was enjoyable, each of them left the restaurant unsure of what might happen next.

CHAPTER SIXTY-SEVEN

Shelly knew Boeing had moved its corporate headquarters to Chicago, but she was surprised to learn how little human resources management remained in Washington, given the number of employees across the state. Her meeting was with Lenore Baker, who oversees all HR activities in Washington.

"Thank you for making yourself available on such short notice, Shelly. I apologize for calling you back multiple times for different interviews. As I mentioned in my email, this happened because some who became familiar with your background had different views on your fit at the company. Things started moving, and the team eventually decided they would like you to consider a different assignment than the one you initially applied for."

"I understand. Boeing is a global company, and things don't always move as quickly as those hoping to join would like. I started to wonder whether anything would come from the meetings, but I'm here now, with you today. I'm grateful for that and look forward to learning what you have in mind for me."

"And with that, I will quickly explain what the alternative position is about. You are right; Boeing is a large company, and because of our size, we don't always have the operational consistency we would like. I can confirm that regarding HR in the greater Seattle area. I am responsible for all HR across the state. I aim to maintain consistency across all plants and offices, adapting to each location's unique realities when necessary. That is a constant challenge. Now, imagine what it's like worldwide. One size doesn't come close to fitting all. Cultural differences, country-specific laws, and communication challenges create issues in managing every aspect of our business. And nowhere is that more evident than in Africa, which brings me to you. You were born in Africa, and while we understand why you want to migrate to the US, we know your cultural background, along with your education in process management, will benefit the companies you work for. We would like you to consider a position tentatively called Director of Process Management, Africa. Just as I find it difficult to manage and coordinate HR throughout the state, anyone trying to do so across all our offices in Africa would face an even greater challenge. The region is so vast, with numerous cultures, languages, rules, and regulations; it seems almost impossible to me," Lenore said, shaking her head to stress the point. "I can't speak to how process management compares to human resources. Whatever the case, it's not an easy task."

"I'm imagining the role you are considering for me. You are right; it would be extremely challenging. One of my university courses involved a week of meetings with process management students from universities in seven countries. We were tasked with defining business process management in each of our countries, reconciling differences, and establishing a comprehensive framework for all companies to follow. You say you struggle to do that across this one state for HR. It borders on the impossible across Africa. However, that was partly due to participants' immaturity, given our age and lack of work experience, as well as some who were more focused on pushing their own views than on working toward a group consensus. I would hope that would be less of a problem in corporations, where workers learn to collaborate."

"You would hope so, but based on my experience as a career HR manager, not as much as it should be. Let me clarify what management hopes this position can ultimately achieve. They don't want or expect a set of process management rules and regulations to be imposed on every Boeing facility, assuming they will be followed precisely. Consensus is important, but it should serve only as a general guide, flexible enough to address the unique circumstances of each facility across Africa. Your role would involve traveling to these companies and subsidiaries, learning how they manage processes, and providing education you believe would benefit them. The military often emphasizes the importance of "going by the book." That's not what we want, nor do we think it would work if such a process management 'book' actually existed. Instead, we want this role to develop a highly adaptable guideline for interpretation by all Boeing's African entities. Does this sound like something you could and would like to do? It's certainly not the position you initially applied for."

Shelly paused before responding.

"Would like to do it, yes; could do it? I'll have to think about that. It will be difficult, at times frustrating, to create such a guide appropriate for such a diverse group of users. How much time do I have to decide?"

"Please think it over. This decision is as important to Boeing as it is to you. If you decide to move forward, there is only one more step I need to share with you. I would like you to visit the corporate office to meet with the three executives whose input led to this offer. You won't be meeting them to seek their approval; you already have that as a result of the interview process. These three executives are primarily interested in ensuring that the person who accepts this role has the best chance of success. They will be your advocates at the highest level of Boeing management."

Shelly smiled, "No pressure, is there, Lenore?"

"None whatsoever. Well, maybe a little when you get there," she smiled back at Shelly. "And no pressure about deciding what you want to do, but can you give me an idea of how much time you'll need to consider it?"

"A day at most. Can I call you tomorrow afternoon?"

"Perfect, Shelly, I look forward to speaking with you tomorrow.

CHAPTER SIXTY-EIGHT

WHILE SHELLY MEANT WHAT SHE SAID ABOUT NEEDING TO CONSIDER THE redefined, expanded position, she also knew she would accept it if the offer details matched the responsibilities. Whatever those details were, she would seek assurances regarding Boeing's promise to help her migrate to the US.

With the long day behind her, physically and emotionally exhausted, Shelly showered and got into bed, telling herself to do what she had said she would do: seriously consider the offer. She was fast asleep within fifteen minutes.

Why are you back, Shelly?

I want confirmation that accepting this position is the right choice for me.

Assurance from me, who knows very little compared with what you know? You are usually very self-assured. Why the hesitation now?

I don't want any more false starts or dead ends. I'm not asking you to guarantee anything; I want to know what you think. If you were in my position, would you do this?

Based on what I know, I would. Very little of what we hope for actually happens. We plan, things change, we make new plans, and in the end, we don't know whether what is is better than what might have been. That's just the way life is in the one life we live, as well as in all the unlived lives we would have lived had we made different choices. You encouraged Eden to follow the light; it is time now for you to do the same.

CHAPTER SIXTY-NINE

THE FLIGHT TO BOEING'S HEADQUARTERS TOOK ABOUT FOUR HOURS. SHELLY specified in her counteroffer that she wanted to be based in Seattle. Lenore told her to expect to be in Chicago at least once a month, with trips lasting three to five days each. All of this was confirmed during her meeting with the three executives in Chicago before she was formally offered the job. Now that she had accepted the company's offer, she focused on finding a place to live in Bellevue, where Lenore was based.

She knows the area; I'll call her first to see what she thinks.

"Good morning, Shelly. I apologize for not getting back to you sooner. I understand your meeting with the three corporate executives went well and that you have accepted our employment offer with the requested changes. We're happy to have you join us. I'm looking forward to working with you and helping however I can."

"It went well, and thank you for everything you've done for me. I have a question for you. I've been living in a month-to-month apartment while going through the interview process. Now that it's complete and I've accepted the position, I want to find a more permanent place, preferably near SeaTac, given the extensive travel I will be doing. I know you are across the lake in Bellevue. I assume I will also need to attend meetings with you. What are your thoughts on Bellevue for me?"

"There are some very nice areas with equally nice apartments, depending on how much you are willing to spend on rent. They are close enough to SeaTac, but getting there can be a slog at times. Similarly, you can live in downtown Seattle if that is your preference. However, navigating traffic to the airport from either location can be a challenge. I appreciate you being willing to live in Bellevue to be close to me and my office." Lenore hesitated before continuing. "But that should not be a primary reason for you to move here. I'll be frank with you if you promise not to share what I tell you with anyone else."

"I won't, Lenore. You have my word."

"Boeing is a great company. Having worked for them, especially in an international role like yours, will be a positive addition to your resume. But one thing about the company is certain: it is not static. Reorganizations, office openings and closings, and people coming and going are all normal, including for me. There's a good chance my office will be closed within the next six months, and I will no longer be with Boeing."

"You may not be with Boeing at all, or just moving to a new job within Boeing?"

"I am looking for alternatives. The company prioritizes employees for new roles when eliminating their previous ones."

"I'm shocked, Lenore. I had no idea you might be leaving the company."

"I understand, Shelly, but I've been with Boeing for almost five years, which is roughly the average for mid- and senior-level managers across all US companies. I've worked in four offices around greater Seattle, reporting to five different bosses. I'm not sure what will happen next, but I don't see much reason for the company to keep me in my current role. That's also my boss's opinion at corporate. She kindly suggested I consider a change, either within the company or elsewhere. This doesn't relate to you just starting your career at Boeing. I only mentioned it to help answer your question about where to live. Choose Bellevue if you want, but not because of its proximity to me or this office. If I stay here, the office stays open, and you live nearby, that's great. But don't rely on that happening."

"Okay, I understand, and I won't speak to anyone about what you've said."

"I know you won't, Shelly. Good luck with your move, wherever it may be. Please let me know when you've figured it out or if you'd like my opinion on what you're considering. I'll be happy to help in any way I can."

With no need to be close to Lenore, limited options for suitable apartments near SeaTac, and her enjoyment of downtown Seattle, Shelly chose an apartment in Belltown. After her move was complete and she started her new job, she focused on work first, her personal time second.

Travel began immediately, with two weeks of strategy and tactics meetings at the corporate office in Chicago to help orient Shelly to her new assignment. This was followed by a month-long trip to Boeing offices in Addis Ababa and Johannesburg, where she met with management to discuss the process management framework she was expected to develop and implement. It didn't take long for Shelly to realize she was entering the "eye" of an extensive corporate management "storm."

CHAPTER SEVENTY

"I'M HAPPY YOU'VE FOUND WHAT SEEMS TO BE THE PERFECT POSITION FOR you, Shelly, but I have to admit I miss our time together. You're rarely here anymore, at least not when we can spend time together."

Shelly exhaled.

"I know, Kathy. I almost laugh at how different this job is from the one I thought I would have. That would have been very routine. I would have had more time for you than you would have wanted to spend with me."

"I doubt it. Boeing's reputation is feast-or-famine. You've been there for a couple of months. What do you think?"

"I haven't met anyone who's been there longer than five years. Those who've been there three years or more frequently change jobs. But that's a good thing. It's easy for companies and their employees to become complacent. The only constant in life is change. You either evolve or die; there's no in-between. I'm home this Saturday—how about you come to Belltown to see my new apartment? We'll have dinner nearby, and you can stay the night. I have a bedroom all set up for you, and we'll find something to do on Sunday."

"Are you sure? That sounds great, but you haven't been there long and haven't had much time for yourself. Are you sure you want me to take up most of your weekend?"

"I wouldn't have offered if I didn't. Yes, I do. I'll expect you late

Saturday morning with your things so you can stay overnight. We'll start with lunch, decide what to do afterward, and go from there."

"Okay, you win, and thanks for making time for me, Shelly. I do appreciate it."

Kathy arrived at Shelly's apartment just before lunch Saturday morning.

"Come in, Kathy. It's so good to see you. You look great. Give me a hug."

Kathy entered, looking around the living room and the kitchen to the left.

"I expected boxes everywhere. How did you finish this so quickly?"

"A lot of late nights and early mornings putting things away. Plus, I didn't have much to unpack—just two suitcases. Everything else I've bought since moving in," Shelly said, picking up Kathy's overnight bag. "Follow me. I'll show you to your room, madam."

Once in the second bedroom, Kathy shook her head, an amazed look on her face.

"I can't believe this, Shelly. You even have the guest bedroom ready for guests? Are you kidding me? I wouldn't be half this prepared for company with only two weeks' notice they were coming, and I'm home full-time."

"I've always performed better when I have less time to get things done. I started with my room, then the kitchen, the living room, and finally this room. It took me a little over two weeks. I only bought what was immediately available. When it arrived, I jumped on it. No time to waste."

"Can I see your room?"

"Certainly, and then we will head out for lunch and maybe do some shopping. I'm still looking for a few decorative accessories."

The afternoon and evening went smoothly for both of them. Kathy worried that Shelly might have outgrown her, given her new job and all the friends she thought Shelly would now have. But Shelly was still the same; they were good friends enjoying each other's company. After dinner, they were back in Shelly's apartment, relaxing, talking, and sharing a bottle of wine.

"You know what I've been doing. What's new with you, Kathy?"

"Nothing much. Aside from tonight's dinner, I'm working on eating healthier. I've joined a gym and have been going most weekdays for at least an hour. I might not look better, but I definitely feel better."

"I noticed the change in you the instant I opened the door. Good for you!"

Kathy looked to the side; her happy expression from a moment ago was now replaced by a somewhat troubled look. "Thank you."

The immediate change in Kathy's demeanor, as if a switch controlling her mood had been flipped, was evident to Shelly. All afternoon, and just moments before, she seemed to be enjoying herself, happy that the two of them were together again, as they often had been before Shelly started her new job.

"Kathy, I can tell something's wrong. What is it?"

Kathy glanced around the room, hesitant to answer Shelly's question. She looked close to tears. Shelly got up from her chair and sat next to her on the couch. Finally unable to hold back, Kathy began to cry.

"It's okay, Kathy. Let it out. Have a good cry. We are friends. I will help you."

Shelly grabbed a box of tissues from the kitchen breakfast nook and handed it to Kathy. Her crying eased, and she wiped away tears from her eyes and cheeks.

"I feel stupid crying like this. It wasn't enough that I took up your weekend; I had to fall apart in front of you, too. What overnight guest does that? I'm sorry, Shelly."

"There's nothing to be sorry for, Kathy. Please tell me what's bothering you."

Kathy let out an awkward, self-conscious laugh—the kind one does when they've been caught trying to hide something. There was no escape for her; Shelly would make her answer.

“I honestly don't know. It's not my physical health. It's not financial. I have a feeling of doom, as if I'm surrounded by darkness. This afternoon with you was so much fun—a real break from my depression.”

“How long have you felt this way? Have you talked to your doctor? Maybe it's physical.”

"I had a complete physical; all the labs are good."

“Have you considered seeing a psychologist or psychiatrist? Maybe they could help you figure out what's bothering you.”

"My doctor suggested a couple of psychologists I could see, but I haven't yet. I keep thinking things will improve, but they haven't. And tonight, without knowing why, my mood just turned on me. I don't know what's happening, Shelly. Maybe I've just become a crazier old woman than when you last saw me."

Kathy looked at Shelly, hoping to lift the pall she had unintentionally cast over their time together before continuing.

“I'll be okay. I promise. These mood swings come and go. I'm tired. If you don't mind, I think it would be best for me to get a good night's sleep. Is that okay with you?”

"Of course, Kathy, sleep helps. I'll bring you a glass of water. Is there anything else I can get you?"

"A couple of whatever pain medicine you have. I have a headache."

They stood up from the couch, and Kathy went to the guest bedroom while Shelly got a glass of water for her. Kathy was unpacking a few things from her bag when Shelly entered the room.

“I am right down the hall. If anything happens tonight—anything at all—knock on my door, and I will sit with you. I'm not asking you to do this, Kathy, I'm telling you. That's what friends do. You would do the same for me. Do you understand? Anything at all.”

"Thank you, Shelly. Please do not worry about me. I will be fine. I promise. See you in the morning. You rest too."

"We will have a great day tomorrow, Kathy. I promise," Shelly said, turning and leaving the room, closing the door behind her.

CHAPTER SEVENTY-ONE

YOU ARE NOT DREAMING, SHELLY, AND YOU KNOW WHAT KATHY WILL DO IF you don't help her. Relive where you were before you took your life. Kathy is there now. Her sense of impending doom, surrounded by darkness, is something you know well. You have not completed your journey. You are in Seattle with Kathy for a reason. Her depression is real; what you do about it is for you to decide. Your growth can only happen when you realize you are trying to prevent others from taking their own lives. If you can't help someone so close to you, who can you help?

What will you do, Shelly?

CHAPTER SEVENTY-TWO

WHETHER IT WAS THE SUN BEGINNING TO CAST LIGHT ACROSS HER BEDROOM or her memory of Kathy's discomfort last night, Shelly wasn't sure. Now awake, she lay in bed, thinking about last night's dream.

My transformation isn't finished. I need to revisit my past to help Kathy. I want to. The question is, how do I help her? Simply telling her everything will be okay won't make it so.

Shelly closed her eyes, drifting back to sleep, quickly feeling herself pulled into the familiar white vortex of Other Worlds. The room reverberated as if struck by thunder. Sound and sight echoes flashed images of Shelly and Kathy, floating freely in the white space. She struggled to convince herself this was only a dream, her eyes shut tight, her ears covered to block out the noise until... silence.

She waited, hoping the oppressive sound would not start again. Hearing nothing, she slowly opened her eyes. The room was empty except for the two overstuffed leather chairs she now knew so well. She sat in one as Kathy's image gradually appeared, a peaceful expression on her face. Once again, she was back in Other Worlds, this time with Kathy.

"Where are we, Shelly? What is this place?" Kathy calmly asked, glancing around the space she now found herself in, searching for answers.

"Other Worlds Coffee is a sanctuary of sorts for those seeking answers to questions they do not know to ask."

"Why did you bring me here?"

"I didn't, Kathy; you came on your own. You can heal yourself, ending the pain you felt last night and have been feeling for some time now."

"How do I do that?"

"Look around the room. Do you see incomplete images of places, people, and situations you recognize as parts of your life?"

"I do. My mother, father, friends, and extended family are all here. You are, too, Shelly."

"We are here because we love you, Kathy. We see you hurting. We want to help you end your pain."

"I plan to end it. You know I will, just as you ended yours."

"I have experienced pain like yours. I took my own life because I felt I had to. But the pain did not end with my mortal life. I was forced to search the multiverse for what my eternal life should be. If I had done nothing, other souls in different places and circumstances would have decided for me. I needed to find an eternity I would choose. I have done that. I now know what my eternal purpose is meant to be. I am here with you now to help you avoid the misfortune I imposed on myself."

"What do I do, Shelly?"

"This is your life, Kathy. You decide what happens next. I promise that whatever you choose, you will not face it alone. If you give up, do nothing, make no decisions, or take your own life, you will have made that choice. Be careful what you decide, including doing nothing at all."

The swirling white interior began to move slowly, then accelerate, as the low-pitched hum grew louder, forcing Kathy to stand. She turned and saw a pinpoint of white light approaching, its size and brightness increasing with each passing second. The last thought she heard came from an unknown voice.

Walk toward the light, Kathy.

CHAPTER SEVENTY-THREE

Shelly got up, took a shower, dressed, and went to the kitchen to make coffee. Not finding Kathy in the living room, she assumed she was still sleeping.

She needs to rest; last night was tough on her and me. And there was no rest once I went to bed. What a dream. I was in a strange white room. Voices asking what I would do. Kathy was there, but not at first. It was a coffee shop, unlike any I had been in before.

Stopping mid-thought, Shelly wondered about the place she and Kathy were in her dream.

But it felt familiar. All white, the walls shifting, me there alone until Kathy arrived, voices speaking to me. That wasn't a dream. That was a nightmare.

Moments later, Kathy entered the kitchen wearing her pajamas, robe, and slippers, smiling at Shelly.

"Good morning, Kathy. You look like you slept well. I really hope you did."

"Oh, yes, I feel so much better. Shelly, I apologize for crying for no reason last night. I won't lie to you. I haven't been feeling well, but I do feel much better this morning."

"I was hoping to hear that. You scared me. Has this happened before?"

"Yes, I have been struggling. I don't know why I felt so bad. I had a dream last night. You were in it. You talked to me, and I listened carefully to what you said. This morning, I feel so much better."

Shelly got up from the couch and headed toward the kitchen, not because she had listened to all Kathy had to say. She didn't want Kathy to see her surprised reaction.

"I'll start breakfast, bacon and eggs, okay?"

"That would be great. I'm hungry. Let me help you."

"No, you are my guest, Kathy. Just sit and relax. How do you like your eggs? I'll bring you coffee black, right?"

"You remember, yes, black. Fix the eggs however you like. I'm not picky."

Shelly returned with a cup of coffee and handed it to Kathy.

"Fifteen minutes or so for the eggs and bacon. You said I was in your dream, talking to you? Probably because of our discussion before you went to bed. Do you remember what I said?"

Shelly turned to walk back to the kitchen to avoid Kathy seeing her expression.

"I don't remember everything you said, but I do recall quite a bit about the room we were in. It was all white—the floors, ceiling, and walls—shifting as if made of liquid. Fragments of images of my family, some friends, and you floated around. Small, like photos someone had torn into tiny pieces."

Kathy paused, trying to recall every detail of her dream.

"It was so vivid. You told me this is my life. I should be careful about what I choose to do. After last night and now hearing about my crazy dream, you probably think I'm crazy."

Shelly faced the cooktop, with bacon frying in one pan, eggs in another. She wasn't focused on making breakfast. She was captivated by Kathy's description of her dream. Staring straight ahead as if in a trance, Shelly didn't hear Kathy walk into the kitchen, set her cup on the counter, or notice the bacon and eggs, now overcooked and smoking.

"Shelly, the bacon is smoking. Your smoke alarm will go off. Shelly?"

Hearing her voice the second time, Shelly quickly looked down at the pans. Smoke rose from the bacon; the eggs were leathery. She moved both pans off the burner, hoping to appear in control.

"Damn, I drifted off thinking about a work project I need to finish. I have more bacon and eggs. I'll start fresh, this time, focusing only on breakfast. I promise," she said, throwing the overcooked eggs and bacon into the sink, placing the pans back on the stove, then reaching into the fridge for more of both.

Not wanting to embarrass her, Kathy poured herself another cup of coffee and sat at the kitchen table, occasionally glancing at Shelly, trying not to appear as though she were staring.

"It happens. My big mistake was leaving bacon cooking on what I thought was a low flame while I stepped away from the kitchen for just a moment. The phone rang. I answered it and completely forgot about the bacon until the smoke alarm went off. I told the person I was talking to I'd call her back, and when I returned to the kitchen, the bacon was on fire in the pan.

"That could have turned out badly," Shelly said, not taking her eyes off her second attempt making breakfast. "Almost done. Could you get the plates out of the cupboard right behind you and the silverware from the drawer below?"

"Sure. I've been looking for something I can do to help you."

Their breakfast done, the dishes washed and put away, Kathy went to her room to shower, dress, and get ready for the day. Shelly poured another cup of coffee and sat in the living room, thinking about Kathy's dream.

That is no coincidence—I could have described her dream. Should I tell her? Two people don't dream the same thing. No, she feels good this morning. Telling her we dreamed the same thing could put her right back where she was.

CHAPTER SEVENTY-FOUR

DRESSED AND READY TO START THEIR DAY, KATHY SUGGESTED THEY TAKE the ferry to Bremerton to explore and have lunch, then head back to Seattle later in the afternoon.

"We have a choice. The ferry takes about an hour, a pleasant trip through a part of Puget Sound you probably haven't seen. I haven't been there in at least five years. We can return the way we came or take my car to explore several small, interesting towns on our way to Bainbridge. Once there, we can take the ferry back to the Seattle Ferry Terminal. If we don't do that today, you should do it one day, with or without me. Those towns have lots of charming shops and great spots for lunch."

"That sounds good. Are you sure you don't mind driving?"

"Not at all. I enjoy driving, especially through those towns. You'll be surprised how rural and pretty they are, so close to downtown Seattle."

"I know the ocean isn't nearby. Will we make it there?"

"We could, but it's far enough away to justify staying overnight before returning. I could have done that if I had brought more clothes. But I doubt you could, given your job and whatever you were thinking about that made you lose track of breakfast."

"No, you're right. It's better to schedule that for another time. But I would like to take the shorter round trip if you're okay with driving."

"That's what we'll do."

On the ferry, Kathy told Shelly more about their options once they arrived in Bremerton. They decided to walk around a bit before heading to Port Gamble, the furthest point northwest of Seattle, while still having time to catch the ferry back to Seattle from Bainbridge.

"Port Gamble is an interesting place. Supposedly, the most haunted town in all of Washington state," Kathy said, watching Shelly for a reaction.

"Haunted, really? Do people actually believe that?"

"Not everyone, but quite a few do." She paused before continuing. "Previous non-believers like me, before I had an experience on one of my trips there."

"You, Kathy? Tell me, what happened?"

"Well, it wasn't a ghost in a white sheet. I was on a group tour of the Walker-Ames house, supposedly the most haunted house in the most haunted town in Washington state. I lagged a little behind the others. I could still see them. I wasn't alone, but they were maybe thirty feet ahead. I was reading a description of the room we were in. The tour guide finished his talk, and everyone in the group except me followed him to the next stop. I was almost finished reading when I felt the light touch of what I assumed was someone's hand on my right shoulder. I heard a voice, no more than a whisper, and I couldn't make out the words. I thought the guide might have come back for me. I turned around quickly. No one was there. The room was empty, and the group was now in the next room, out of my sight. A chill went down my spine. I hurried to join them and did not fall behind again."

"Oh my, a chill just ran down my spine. What will happen when we're actually there? Don't tell me, Kathy. I don't want to know."

They arrived in Bremerton, parked Kathy's car, and the two of them walked around town, spending less time than they had planned. They decided to keep going, having lunch along the way or when they reached Port Gamble. At one point, the conversation slowed, giving Kathy a moment to focus on her driving while Shelly reflected on how they had both dreamed the same thing.

And now I'm headed to a haunted town. I don't believe in paranormal sightings or sounds, but I have to admit, Kathy's story and our dreams last night have me wondering.

They decided to have lunch in Port Gamble, giving them more time to explore the shops and area surrounding downtown before visiting the Walker-Ames house.

"I can't stop thinking about your experience in that house, Kathy. How did you not scream when you felt a touch on your shoulder?"

"I don't know. I shook when I realized I was alone. I'm not exaggerating. I felt something—or someone—touch me."

"And you just made me shudder again. Let's plan to stay together, shall we?"

"You couldn't peel me away from you if you tried," Kathy said, smiling at Shelly.

Their visit to the Walker-Ames house ended without any unusual incidents for either of them. They started the drive back to Bainbridge and the ferry that would take them to downtown Seattle. As on the way to Port Gamble, their conversation about what they had seen and done soon ended, leaving each of them deep in thought. Shelly again wondered whether she should tell Kathy about their dreams.

What would that accomplish? Since there's no explanation for what I know is true, why should I burden Kathy with something neither of us can explain?

Back in Seattle, they treated themselves to a lobster dinner at one of the many restaurants overlooking Puget Sound, enjoying each other's company, their meal, and a bottle of wine as the sun set behind the snow-capped Olympic Mountains.

"What a great day, Kathy! Thank you for the suggestions and, even more, for spending time with me this weekend."

"I enjoyed it too, Shelly. You are a wonderful friend, and you proved it again this weekend. I wouldn't have done any of this alone. I have other friends who would go with me, but we've done it so many times that we take it for granted. Watching you experience it for the first time made it feel new for me again."

Back at Shelly's apartment, Kathy packed her belongings, preparing to leave. Both felt a bit sad, knowing Shelly's busy travel schedule would cut into the time they could spend together on weekends like this one. They promised to get together as often as possible. Shelly, now alone in her apartment, reflected on the weekend, including Kathy being upset and the fact that they had both essentially dreamed the same thing.

Nothing happened at the haunted house. There was no need for it to; it had already happened here.

She was sure it wasn't a coincidence; they had shared a similar, possibly the same, dream. But she also realized it bothered her a lot less now than when she was making breakfast.

There's nothing I can do about it, no one to talk to about it, certainly not Kathy. I will accept it and move on.

CHAPTER SEVENTY-FIVE

DRIVING HOME, KATHY REFLECTED ON HOW UPSET SHE HAD BEEN AT Shelly's the night before.

Out of nowhere, I lose control of my emotions. I start crying. I could have told Shelly what I'd been thinking about doing. I'm glad I didn't; she would worry even more than she is tonight. Have I really thought enough about killing myself? I wasn't faking it when I told her I felt so good this morning. The best in a long time. But there's still something I need to figure out. I don't know what it is, and I'm unsure how to find out. But I will, and soon.

Once home, tired from the weekend, Kathy took a shower, went to bed, and fell asleep quickly.

Do you remember me telling you that I did what you are thinking about doing? It wasn't a solution for me, and it won't be for you either. Learn from your dreams—they are often memories of a life you could have lived had you made different choices in the past. They serve as warnings, urging you to think carefully before you act; they hint at a future you might want to avoid.

I took my own life, Kathy, because the man I loved was killed fighting in a war he didn't willingly join. I couldn't bear to live without him, not even knowing for sure he was dead. We would have been married and had a daughter named Eden. That never happened, but I did meet Eden and was briefly reunited with Raymond, who would have been my husband. We would have been Eden's parents.

You may one day understand what some of your unlived lives could have been like if you hadn't taken your own life. Only a few do, and having been one of them, I'm uncertain whether we who survive are blessed or cursed. But I know this: if you end your life, your soul will be lost in the multiverse, as mine still is. The difference now is that I know my purpose. I exist to help others avoid what I went through by sharing my story. You and I connect so well because I am here to share my experience with you. I want to help you avoid the mistake I made. I can't force you to do what I say or even consider it, but it is my destiny to try.

Very soon, you will face a choice that requires careful consideration before you decide what to do. Recognize that not *deciding, whether consciously or not, is itself a choice. You will have questions that require answers. You will never have all the answers, yet you are still compelled to choose. If you fail to decide, others and outside circumstances will make that decision for you. Do not let that happen. You have all the knowledge you need to determine your ultimate eternal fate.*

You will soon meet others, all of whom, in different ways, are here to help you. Trust that they are, and accept their help. You have been to Other Worlds; you will again soon. You have experienced the loss of friends and family. You have seen the white light calling you to enter. Walk toward the light, Kathy; it is your path to immortality. It will teach you what you need to know before making the one choice that will define your eternal existence in one of an infinite number of universes within the multiverse.

You need to know all of this to recognize when it is time to leave a place, person, or situation. Do not minimize the importance of what you choose. Do not put off changing something you know is wrong for you. Doing so is a decision the consequences of which will end your ability to choose your immortal life.

CHAPTER SEVENTY-SIX

AS HAD HAPPENED SO OFTEN RECENTLY, KATHY WOKE UP MORE EXHAUSTED than when she had gone to bed. Not physically, but emotionally and mentally, as if she had spent the night confronting a problem she could not solve.

My God, another night of endless dreams I remember little of this morning. When will it end? I can't continue like this. Night after night, the only rest I've gotten has been at Shelly's, and even that came only after I broke down in front of her. What did she say that helped me so much? There's something about this in my life; I need to be careful about what I choose. I dreamed that, too. Shelly was in that dream.

In a split-second flash, Kathy recalled a part of her dream from her night at Shelly's apartment.

Shelly was in my dream last night, and the one at her apartment. She is the key to helping me understand my dreams. They are so clear to me when I am asleep, but not when I wake up. She will know why. I shouldn't bother her during the week, but I have no choice. I must ask her to help me. If I don't...

"Good morning, Carla. How was your weekend?"

"Fine, nothing special. Took the kids to their soccer games, did a little housework while Ed took the car in for new tires. Pretty boring, huh?"

"Anything done too often can become boring. You can at least take comfort in knowing you're doing what you should for your kids. That, and it's Ed sitting at the tire place waiting to get the car back. I'm at SeaTac with about an hour before my flight. Any messages before I board?"

"Only one. Kathy called about an hour ago, no last name. She said she needs to talk to you. I told her I thought you might already be in the air and that I would pass along the message when you landed. She sounded upset."

This was not something Shelly wanted to hear. She had-much to do when she arrived at corporate regarding her previous meeting at Boeing's office in Addis Ababa.

This better not require me to go back to Africa. I was just there for ten days three weeks ago. Why couldn't whatever this is have happened then?

She looked at her watch before responding.

"Okay, Carla, I will call her before I board. Thank you."

"She left a number. Do you want it?"

"No, I have it, thanks."

Shelly hung up and dialed Kathy.

"Hello."

"Kathy, this is Shelly. I just got your message. I need to board my flight in about twenty minutes. Are you okay?"

"Oh, Shelly, thank you so much for calling. I apologize for bothering you, but there was no one else who could help me. I had another terrible night. I can't remember the details of my dream, but it wasn't good. I woke up feeling as depressed as I ever have. But then I realized you were in my dream the night I stayed with you. I'm sure whatever you said helped me feel much better the next day. And here's the strange part. Realizing that you were in it made me certain you were in last night's dream as well. I don't recall what it was about, but I know you were a part of it. Can you think of anything that might help me make sense of all this? I hate to say this..."

She paused long enough for Shelly to know what she would say whether she said it or not.

"Kathy, listen to me carefully. Don't do anything rash. You don't know enough about what's happening to make a decision that will affect the rest of your life. I'm about to leave and won't be back for at least two, maybe three weeks. I can call you later today after my meetings at corporate. But as soon as they're finished, I may have to leave for an emergency meeting in Addis Ababa. If that weren't the case, I would come to help you handle whatever is going on. I can't do that now. Think back to our weekend together. You told me the morning after that first night at my apartment that I had been in your dream the night before. You said you couldn't remember what I said, but it made you feel better when you woke up. Think about your dreams, try to remember what they were about. Do you understand what I'm telling you, Kathy?"

"I do, Shelly. It makes sense, and I feel better hearing you reassure me. I will do my best to follow your instructions. I know you have to go. Don't worry about me. I will be here when you get back. Have a safe trip."

"You've promised, so don't let me down, Kathy. I'm not there with you, but I'll be watching from afar. I will call you later this evening, my time, if possible. If you don't hear from me, it's because I'm still in meetings. Okay?"

"Yes, Shelly. Thank you again. Goodbye."

The call ended, and Shelly knew she had to board after hearing her name called twice while on the phone with Kathy. She hurried to the plane, found her seat, and settled in for the four-plus-hour flight to Chicago. When she arrived, she went to the office for meetings to prepare for whatever was happening in Addis Ababa.

Having told Kathy she should try to recall her dreams, Shelly couldn't think of anything else to tell her to do or not do. She knew what Kathy had dreamed in her apartment; she had the same dream herself.

I know what she meant when she said, 'I will be here when you get back.' She won't be if I don't act now.

CHAPTER SEVENTY-SEVEN

SHELLY'S MEETING AT CORPORATE RAN WELL INTO THE NIGHT, TOO LATE FOR Shelly to call Kathy.

What would I have said if I had called? Just offering more encouragement, code for 'Don't kill yourself, Kathy, at least not before I can be there.'

Back in her hotel room, she took off her shoes and lay down on the bed, feeling physically relieved after a nearly five-hour flight followed by a three-hour meeting. But emotionally, she felt as drained as Kathy had been when they had talked earlier in the day. Soon after, she fell asleep.

You were right to seek help, Shelly. Kathy will not wait for you to arrive.

She felt mentally and physically relaxed, as she often did when back in Other Worlds. But not always. There were times when she had to face reality she tried—and failed—to ignore. But she always found answers to questions she hadn't known to ask. She was confident this time would be no different.

She opened her eyes and realized she was no longer on the bed in her Chicago hotel room. Instead, she was back in Other Worlds, sitting comfortably in the same overstuffed leather chair she had occupied every time she visited before, a cup of hot black coffee on the table beside her. It was the familiar Other Worlds she knew so well. No windows, no doors, no other tables or chairs, or people. She reached for the coffee, feeling the heat radiate from the cup. She lifted it to her lips, feeling steam rising from the coffee. In any other coffee shop, that steam and heat would warn her that the coffee was too hot to sip. But not here, not in Other Worlds. She took a sip; the temperature was just right.

What now, Shelly?

Kathy must be here with me.

That's why you're here. No one called you; you know you need to be here. You understand your role. But do you know what to do?

Shelly hesitated before responding, remembering that in Other Worlds, there were no secrets; her thoughts were known to everyone.

She's here because she needs to be. My role is to guide her.

Yes, and because of that, your paths are more deeply intertwined than you realize. Her presence is an opportunity, not an obstacle, for both of you. Kathy is asking for your help for herself and for you, Shelly. If you can't save her, you will not save yourself.

Is it time?

You know.

Kathy wanted to follow Shelly's suggestion: *set aside what troubles me and focus on recalling my dream. Why not? I have nothing more important than this. I will try.*

She returned to her room, made her bed, and, standing there looking at it, decided to lie down and try to focus on the good that came from the dream she had in Shelly's apartment.

Walk toward the light, Kathy; it guides you to immortality. It will reveal what you still need to learn before making the one choice that determines your eternal existence in one of countless universes within the multiverse.

Once again, the low-register hum grew louder, the pinhole light brighter and larger, holding her tightly. She saw fragments of floating images of her family and friends. The walls, ceilings, and floors appear seamless and calm on the surface while moving beneath. Faint at first, the images now grew clearer. She saw Shelly sitting in an overstuffed leather chair across from her.

"Kathy, this moment not only determines what remains of your mortal life but also what will define your eternal existence."

"What is left of my mortal life? Am I not already dead?"

"You are not. You stand at a crossroads, a symbol of the choice you must make between life and death. The path you choose will determine whether you die or live forever. I know you are confused and unsure about what is being asked of you and what you need to know to make a confident choice. I am here to help with that. My mortal life ended when I took my own life. You know me as mortal because our relationship occurs in one of the lives you would have lived if you had made different choices in the past. This is a temporary stop for you—a brief place to think about what you want to do. Your options will become clear and simple once you understand what leads to each. My role is to help you discover what that is."

"You are dead. I am not, but I might be soon, depending on what I choose, correct?"

"Yes, I am with you as an immortal."

"How do I learn?"

"Walk to the light; it will take you to my mortal end."

Kathy remained seated in her chair, her eyes tightly closed as the hum grew louder. As before, a pinpoint light appeared, small at first, expanding until it enveloped her completely. She felt weightless, surrounded by the floating, fragmentary images of family and friends she had seen during both visits to Other Worlds. She accepted this was all meant to help her. The hum stopped, and she felt the light holding her tightly just moments before releasing her. She opened her eyes to find herself in a place she did not recognize.

You are with me in my apartment in Zimbabwe long before you knew me, as you believe you do now. I was mortal then, living unhappily as you are today. I saw little point in continuing to live my life as it was. Does that sound familiar, Kathy? Watch the end of my mortality—a day when I stood at my crossroads, just as you now stand at yours. Afterward, tell me whether you think my reasoning for what I was about to do was sound.

Shelly suddenly woke up, sitting upright, staring into the distance, seeing nothing. She knew a conversation had replaced her dream, but she couldn't tell who she was talking to.

A *conversation with myself? It has to be that. Call it a dream, a premonition. I'm not sure. I'm not talking to anyone but myself. But if that's true, what am I telling myself to do? I know what I'm thinking: is that what I really want?*

Shelly spent the rest of her day and into the night thinking only about her dream. She questioned her thoughts, wondering whether they were separate from her or merely something her mind created. She concluded that either way, it did not matter.

It was not as if she hadn't considered all possibilities; she had thought about them extensively over several months. She was unhappy in Zimbabwe. She had few legal options for migrating to where she might want to live. What would be the point of trading one unhappy life for another? She enjoyed parts of her dreams, especially those about traveling, hoping to find an alternative life. But even that left her feeling empty. There was someone in her dream, a young man on a beach. She had good feelings about him, though she could not remember what he looked like or even his name.

I can't take it anymore! I know what I need to do, and now is the time. I might be dreaming, but I can't tell, and I don't care. I'm ending this insanity right now!

Shelly got up from the couch and walked to the desk beside her bed. Opening the drawer, she took out a shoebox, carefully placing it on the desk, the lid beside it. She paused, looking at the contents of the box as she had many times before.

But I am now certain this is what I must do. This is the solution I have been searching for.

Shelly took the gun out of the box, put it to her forehead, and pulled the trigger.

———

"Open your eyes, Kathy."

Kathy obeyed the voice's command, a voice she did not recognize. She found herself once again seated in her chair in Other Worlds, with Shelly sitting across from her, beside an Asian man Kathy didn't know, who was standing off to the side. She heard the same voice instructing her to open her eyes.

"Shelly asked you to witness the end of her mortal life. She requested that you listen to her reasoning for doing so, so you could decide whether you agree with what she did and said. You have now seen the end of Shelly's mortal life. You have heard her reasoning for what she was about to do. Did she choose to do the right thing?"

When the Asian stranger stopped talking, Kathy quickly turned her head toward Shelly, believing she couldn't have done so while he was speaking. Shelly looked at Kathy, her expression revealing nothing of what she was thinking. Kathy looked at the Asian man, then back at Shelly, neither of them speaking, their eyes fixed on Kathy. She knew they were waiting for her to respond.

"Shelly, I don't understand why you decided to take your own life. Because you had limited legal options to migrate to a place you'd want to live? Or because your dreams left you feeling empty? Neither justifies taking your life. No, I do not agree with your reasoning at that moment."

Kathy breathed an audible sigh of relief.

"You shouldn't have, Kathy. All I did and thought that afternoon was wrong. I created a false justification for my actions. I know that now, and I have suffered for it ever since. But I received a second chance that could change what would otherwise be my eternal existence. Like me, you are at a crossroads and must decide what you will do. However, unlike me, you can avoid making an unalterable mistake. You came here believing you could no longer live with the pain you feel. You told yourself you had done everything possible to understand the cause of that pain, doing what was necessary to stop it. But that was not true; you were ready to do as I did. You were ready to stop trying. Now you know everything there is to know, Kathy. Now you can go back to the life you were living, choosing to identify and eliminate the source of your pain. Or you can decide to do as I did and stop trying."

Kathy listened carefully to Shelly.

"Will I know what to do?"

"Not if you stop trying."

Once again, Kathy heard the Asian stranger's voice, compelling her to look at him.

"It is time for you to return to your life, Kathy. When you do, you must choose that which will shape the rest of your mortal life and the beginning of your immortal future. Choose carefully."

AFTERWORD

What did Kathy choose to do? What happens to Raymond, Asian, Shelly, Eden, An, and all the other unlived characters? We all have an infinite number of lives we could have lived; there must be more to this than these three books!

Ten years ago, I had a vague idea of what has since become the Unlived Lives Trilogy. What if someone were to encounter themselves at a high school reunion, meeting their doppelgängers who had made different choices after high school than they had? Or maybe a person looking in a mirror who sees a very different version of themself based on their past choices. They could swap places with the alternative in the mirror, "visiting" some of their unlived lives.

What would it be like for a person to learn that they had been dead for a long, long time, existing in the multiverse alongside an infinite number of their doppelgängers who had made an endless number of different choices, each leading to different outcomes and lives?

I want to say I carefully considered how all this might become the basis for the three Unlived books, but I can't. Instead, I found myself dreaming an endless number of storylines and characters in a variety of situations and countries, many of which I had visited. People living and dead learning they had the option to "visit" some of the lives they could have lived had they made different choices.

What would that be like?

Given the chance, would someone who died choose to visit lives they could have lived? If so, how would they decide which lives? Does how happy someone is in the life they lead determine whether they would choose to experience an alternative life they could have lived?

The beginning of all of this really starts with the Many-Worlds Interpretation debate, the shortest summary of which is:

> ***In 1957, American physicist Hugh Everett III challenged the status quo with the Many-Worlds Interpretation. He proposed a universe where the wave function is an objective reality that never collapses, but instead branches into a sprawling multi-verse of every possible physical outcome.***

If your eyes glossed over reading that, try this.

Proponents of the theory hold that every choice and decision you make throughout your life results in another "you" who made the opposite choice or decision now existing in a parallel universe to the one you inhabit.

(Note to science nerds who, having read the Many-Worlds summary, now feel the need to argue any of the above. Don't bother. It's not what my books are about, and we both have more important things to do.)

Do you dare?

Eden, the daughter of Raymond and Shelly who was never born, first appeared in *Reckoning*. You know who your children are. Have you ever wondered about the children you would have had if you made different choices in the past?

I've asked people who comment on or ask questions about the characters in the Unlived Lives stories whether they would like to visit some of their unlived lives. Without fail, several say they would not, because they do not want to lose the family and friends they have in the life they do live.

I answer: *"You are only visiting lives you would have lived, some of which will include family and friends in the life you do live."*

That's not sufficiently comforting for some, but not for the reasons I assumed. Some are less concerned about losing their current family than they are about not knowing what the family in a different life would be like.

For them, the devil they know is preferred to the one they don't know.

What would you do?

Imagine having access to an "Unlived Life mirror." Standing before it, you see yourself living your current life. *If* you choose to do so, you can step through the mirror to visit your doppelgänger without them being aware of your presence. An out-of-body opportunity to see what one of the lives you would have lived would be like. The differences between the two could be few to many, with outcomes somewhat to very different from your life. You may like some of what you find, as well as some things you don't, including yourself.

I can list several versions of my unlived lives based on the choices I made and didn't make. Some I like; others I don't. No one is perfect. Mistakes are part of our development. If you don't believe that applies to you, ask your spouse, siblings, kids, a parent, another relative who knows you, or a friend whose opinion you value to comment on you. If they are honest, be prepared to hear things about yourself you don't like. We never stop making mistakes. The best we can do is learn from them to avoid repeating them, leaving room to make new ones.

The consequences of most of our mistakes are not serious; we can rectify them with a simple "my bad" and an apology. But that isn't always the case. Seemingly inconsequential actions and words can place you in a life you never imagined living, good or bad. When that happens, the image in the mirror *is* your life, one you cannot change.

I've tried to write interesting stories about individuals experiencing their unlived lives. Some are dead; one was never born; one is alive—all caught up in the web of uncertainty between mortality and immortality. Their stories unfold around the world, across different periods of time, on almost every continent, in places real and imagined. If you have read all three Unlived Lives books and found yourself "seeing" these people and places, you can also "see" yourself in your own unlived lives. The question is, will you choose to do that?

Future Unlived Lives.

"All things must pass."

I could list many emotions to describe my time writing, editing, publishing, and marketing the Unlived Lives Trilogy. It began with me having little idea what I was doing. I was writing a book, but I didn't know how to make it successful or even how to define success. If you are an aspiring "author" who has recently written or will soon write a book, this may describe you, too. Whatever the case, do not assume you will make money doing it. Spend money, yes; make money, probably not. Do it for reasons personal to you.

I've written and self-published four books:

- *The 7 Keys to Change*
- *The Unlived Lives of Raymond Quinn*
- *The Unlived Lives of Shelly Bennett*
- *The Unlived Lives: Reckoning*

7 Keys was a "calling card" for my consulting practice. I never expected it to sell many copies, and it lived up to that expectation. I gave it to clients I hoped would see value in my approach to change management, with some retaining me for follow-on services. It did that, with all the costs associated with producing it covered by just one of numerous consulting assignments that followed.

The Unlived trilogy is an entirely different story.

7 Keys is nonfiction. *Unlived Lives* is fiction. The only way to break even, much less make money writing fiction, is to sell a lot of books. Sales of Unlived Lives books to date have significantly exceeded my expectations. Time will tell what the financial outcome will be. Time will also tell whether there will be any future Unlived Lives books, which brings me to the following.

My time writing Unlived Lives stories is over. On any given day, I have enjoyed or hated the process, which now ends with the trilogy I never intended to write.

However, that does not mean there will be no future Unlived Lives books. There will be, just as there were books with similar themes before my books came along. The only question is, who will write them?

The Unlived Lives concept is simple. You can live only one life, but you have an infinite number of unlived lives.

Most of you reading this will have read all three Unlived Lives books. Where would you take their story? You can probably imagine many possible storylines, not all of which would be worth pursuing. But you only need one to continue the Unlived Lives saga.

You can write future Unlived Lives books, and if you are interested, I can help you.

The characters in my Unlived Lives trilogy are mine. They come from my imagination; I own them. If you like the Unlived Lives concept and have an idea where to take it in the future, creating new characters in storylines completely different from mine, go for it! Expand the concept; you don't need my permission or my characters to do that. But if you would like to take Raymond, Shelly, Asian, and some or all of the others on new adventures, let's talk.

Not a writer?

Do you believe writers are the only people who have written and published books?

Writers write, and nothing should stop you from writing, including you. If you want to write and believe you would enjoy continuing the Unlived Lives series I've created, let's talk.

I have nothing to sell you. I will not ask you for money. I will judge you on your ability to continue the Unlived Lives series. I will explain the process of writing and publishing books, along with the cost. With that information, you can decide whether Unlived Lives will be a part of your future.

For more information about the Unlived Lives trilogy and me, visit williammatthies.com

ACKNOWLEDGMENTS

Thanks to the many readers who took a chance on an unknown author. I am grateful.

I spent eight years writing and rewriting *The Unlived Lives of Raymond Quinn*. I'd only ever written magazine articles and a nonfiction book, so storytelling stretched (and sometimes sprained) new muscles. I figured I had one novel in me and I'd better get it out of my head and onto the page. I released Raymond to the world in 2024.

Turns out I'm not the only one fascinated by "what could have been." Thousands of readers purchased my first novel. Many readers emailed me or posted on my Facebook Page. One question popped up repeatedly: What happens next?

You'd think writing a second novel would be easier than the first. You would be wrong. I created a world; now I had to keep it spinning.

The Unlived Lives of Shelly Bennett was published in 2025, and now *The Unlived Lives: Reckoning* completes the trilogy.

Or does it? Perhaps these characters soldier on in an alternate universe in stories written by a different William Matthies. Or written by you? (See Afterword.)

Thanks to **Flo Selfman** for her meticulous proofreading of this story and her gentle corrections. And to **JT Farrell** for his outstanding narration on all three books.

Finally, a special thanks to **Paula Johnson** for designing all three covers and my website and handling the dozens of tasks required to publish each novel. She's creative, organized, and just the right amount of bossy. When we first worked together at a start-up 40-plus years ago, neither one of us had "publishing novels about parallel universes" on our bingo cards.

ABOUT THE AUTHOR

Like his Raymond Quinn character, William Matthies served in the U.S. Army, including a year-long stint in Vietnam with B Battery, 2nd Battalion, 19th Airborne Artillery, 1st Cavalry Division during the war. After the service, he graduated from college, married, raised two sons, and eventually found his true calling as a serial entrepreneur.

His most recent venture involved teaching the art and science of change management to organizations and individuals. His book, *The 7 Keys to Change,* is based on several years of research on how to manage both personal and professional change.

Pushing the envelope is second nature to Matthies. At 13, he and a friend embarked on a solo voyage to Catalina Island off the California coast. Their goal was a parent-free campout, but the result was a lifetime ban from the island.

That didn't stop him from visiting another island many years later, riding a bike from one end of Cuba to the other.

Matthies continues to seek out experiences to alter his perspective, including a Mach 2.5 flight in a MiG 25 supersonic Russian aircraft departing from Zhukovsky Air Base outside of Moscow.

He plays guitar in his spare time and has maintained absolute beginner status for more than three decades.

Matthies has yet to experience an alternate life while fully expecting to any day now.

www.ingramcontent.com/pod-product-compliance
Lightning Source LLC
LaVergne TN
LVHW010646110826
845149LV00014B/2971

* 9 7 9 8 9 9 0 9 9 8 6 4 3 *